'Are you mad?' he yelled as he pulled the hat free. 'I'm already freezing and now you cover me in oil...what the hell is up with you?'

He stopped his rant the moment her warm fingers began working the oil all over his cold muscled chest. He looked down to see both of her hands moving slowly but purposefully across his bare skin. He raised his gaze to look at her beautiful face. Suddenly his emotions took over and he took her wrists with his hands. He said nothing, searching her eyes for a reaction, before he pulled her up against his body and kissed her.

She froze as he pressed his lips down on hers, then unwillingly she melted into his kiss. A moment before he had been so angry, but now his lips met hers there was no anger. His kiss was tender and passionate. For a brief moment she relished being that close to him. The desire he was stirring within her was undeniable and it felt so good. She didn't want it to end.

But she had to pull away.

'No...we can't.' She struggled to speak as she could still taste his mouth on hers. Her heart was racing as she pulled her emotions into line and her body away from his.

He released her immediately. 'It was just a kiss, I wasn't about to throw you onto the ground and ravage you in the crops...not yet, at least.'

Dear Reader

In my third book, FALLING FOR DR DECEMBER, I am thrilled to introduce you to the New England town of Uralla, located three hundred miles north of Sydney. The name originates from a local Aboriginal word *'oorala'*, meaning 'a camp' or 'a place where people come together', and it is where my brother and his family live.

Late last year, the wedding of my very handsome nephew Myles to his gorgeous fiancée Anne gave me the opportunity to travel to Uralla and experience a true country wedding. Myles—along with my other equally handsome nephews, and his groomsmen Ben and Eric—would be more than suited to the role of my hero, the tall, dark and handsome Dr Pierce Beaumont!

The wedding reception was held in a farm building on the Samaurez Homestead property and it was one of the loveliest I have ever attended. Dancing on a cobblestone floor, open paddocks surrounding the celebrations, and gingham-trimmed jam keepsakes were just a part of an unforgettable evening.

The town inspired me to write FALLING FOR DR DECEMBER as I wanted to capture the wonderful feeling of a close-knit, caring community like Uralla. It is a town where you literally do not have to lock your front door because everyone in the street is either family or friend.

I hope you fall in love with the town and the people as you read the heart-warming story of Laine Phillips and Dr Pierce Beaumont.

Warmest wishes

Susanne

FALLING FOR DR DECEMBER

BY
SUSANNE HAMPTON

First published in Great Britain 2014
by Mills & Boon, an imprint of Harlequin (UK) Limited,
Eton House, 18-24 Paradise Road, Richmond, Surrey, TW9 1SR

© 2014 Susanne Panagaris

ISBN: 978-0-263-24356-7

Married to the man she met at eighteen, **Susanne Hampton** is the mother of two adult daughters—one a musician and the other an artist.

The family also extends to a slightly irritable Maltese shih-tzu, a neurotic poodle, three elderly ducks and four hens that only very occasionally bother to lay eggs. Susanne loves everything romantic and pretty, so her home is brimming with romance novels, movies and shoes.

With an interest in all things medical, her career has been in the dental field and the medical world in different roles, and now Susanne has taken that love into writing Mills & Boon® Medical Romance™.

Recent titles by Susanne Hampton:

BACK IN HER HUSBAND'S ARMS
UNLOCKING THE DOCTOR'S HEART

**These books are also available in eBook format
from www.millsandboon.co.uk**

Dedication

To my wonderful family who call the
town of Uralla home—Greg, Tracy, Myles,
Anne, Ben, Eric, Emma, Poppy and Bob.

To their friends in Uralla and Armidale
for being so warm and friendly, just as you imagine
country people to be.

You live in a beautiful part of Australia
and I hope I have done the town justice.

CHAPTER ONE

'JUST ONE MORE step and I'll shoot!' Laine waited for some reaction, but there was nothing.

The man before her appeared unmoved by her words. He stood in silence, shaking his head, his dark, deeply set eyes staring back coldly. The clenched muscles of his jaw made his face appear even more angular and harsh. Laine was painfully aware that he had no intention of taking her seriously. *But why would he?* Her willowy stature would pose no threat to his potent six-foot frame now stripped bare to the waist. He wasn't about to listen to her plea.

The afternoon sun slipped through the curtain breaks and she watched the curves of his broad chest and powerful arms etched by the light. Slowly he ran his fingers over his open belt buckle. She felt the need to swallow as his fingers moved to the top stud of his jeans. Her eyes closed for the briefest moment but opened just as quickly. She hoped it was not more than a blink. Showing any sign of intimidation she was feeling would give him the upper hand. She had learned that over the years.

'I promise, take another step and it'll be your last,' Laine called aloud, while silently she chided herself for having been talked into coming back here in the first place. *Why had she done it?* She should have known no good would come from returning to this town. The lump in her throat that had formed when she'd driven her hire car down the New England Highway and into Uralla that morning showed no sign of being swallowed. It was lodged firmly and going nowhere. It was a sign she should not be here. She had left the town twelve years ago for good reason.

She waited for his response in action or words but there was nothing. He showed no emotion. She couldn't read his face. Instead she felt the weight of his gaze as it roamed her body, slowly, painstakingly, making her feel uneasy with every lingering moment, until it came to rest on her mouth. Running his hand through his short black hair, he appeared distracted as he stared at her in silence. Then abruptly his husky voice made her stiffen as he asked brazenly, 'You really know how to use that?'

Only able to catch his unshaven profile, she could see his mouth curve into a smirk. She fought his intimidation with all her strength. She refused to let him know he was close to succeeding in his desire to unnerve her. She had to maintain the upper hand and stay in control and that meant staying calm.

'Take that step and you'll soon find out how accurate I can be.' Her tone was mild and steady, even though inside she wavered. Laine hoped her newfound composure, albeit at odds with her true feelings, might prove more successful. She knew this was the last time she could issue her ultimatum without it echoing as an empty threat. She would not get what she'd come for and all of this would have been for nothing. No one was going to get the better of her. Not here and not now.

She held her ground and prayed this time he'd take her seriously. And he did. Grudgingly, and with a level of hesitation Laine didn't fully understand, he set his dusty boots up another rung of the ladder and eased his long leg over the top to sit astride it.

'At last,' she muttered to herself as she tucked some stray wisps of her long brown hair behind her ear and reached for another lens from the table behind her. With her camera focused, and maintaining eye contact with her handsome but obstinate subject, Laine moved behind the ladder prop and began a photographic shoot with the confidence and expertise that only someone with her ability and experience could execute.

A cold sweat rushed over Pierce but he swallowed hard and kept his eyes from looking down. His heart was pounding roughly in his chest as he struggled to push unwanted images from his mind. Memories were rising to the surface and no matter how logic reasoned with his fear, fear was close to taking hold. Despite the fact that he wasn't that twelve-year-old boy balancing precariously on a balcony ledge, he suddenly found himself feeling equally vulnerable. His knuckles clenched whitely and he willed the shoot to be over. Nervously he rubbed his brow. He had to stay on task, remind himself it was just a ladder in an unused consulting room of his practice in order to maintain any remnant of composure. He knew it wouldn't be easy when he took the first step, but he hadn't expected it to be so overwhelming all these years later. Some memories were clearly hard, if not impossible, to forget.

'You can come down now but seriously, Dr. Beaumont, was that so terribly difficult?' she asked with exaggerated politeness, as she removed the lens and packed the camera body back into its case. 'If you'd gone up another rung without the dramatics, we could have wrapped up twenty minutes ago,' she complained as she began to dismantle the lighting umbrella. She was tempted to comment further on his bad attitude but didn't want to cause any more animosity. Better to keep her opinion to herself, she mused as she began packing the tripod in the longest of her waterproof equipment bags.

Pierce Beaumont couldn't answer her. He climbed down from the ladder in silence. With both feet on solid ground, anxiety morphed to anger. 'What was so damned important about going up one more step?'

'It's about framing the picture. I won't compromise when it comes to my work. And please don't be late tomorrow. I'm hoping to get the sunrise over the McKenzies' property,' she replied flatly, as she glared back at the man who had made the last hour very difficult. 'I've already photographed eleven other GPs across Australia and you have been without doubt the most uncooperative. Why on earth agree in the first place if you don't want to see yourself in a calendar? I saw the contract, it was clearly your name and signature on it.'

'That's just it,' he snapped back. 'I didn't agree to any of this. My former partner, Gregory Majors, forged the paperwork before he retired. He did it as a prank. Thought I'd see the humour in it. Clearly, I didn't.'

Laine knew the name instantly. Dr Majors, the town's general practitioner. It was a name that brought memories rushing back at lightning speed. It was something he would do. The man had an impish side to him. Laine had been his patient many times when she'd lived in Uralla. The first time when she'd come down with tonsillitis, then there had been her broken arm from a fall during a high-school netball game and a few other teenage scrapes. He had been the local doctor since he'd finished medical school when, like so many of the townspeople, he'd come back to nest.

But not Laine. She had left and vowed never to return. She took a deep breath. The time that she had called Uralla her home was over and she could never think of it that way again. She had planned it would be her forever home but that dream had ended and taken with it her belief in the words 'for ever'.

'When I tried to back out of it, the organisers told me that they'd booked your flights and the budget wouldn't allow them to reschedule,' Pierce continued, bringing Laine back from her reverie. 'I offered to pay for new flights for you to wherever they could find another mug who'd agree to take my place but apparently they couldn't find anyone. They explained that the entire timeline would have blown out and they wouldn't have met the deadline. No calendar meant there'd be no fundraising for next year. They played the guilt card very well.'

There was more to it than that. Pierce hadn't been able to walk away after he had read the charity prospectus and realised what a worthwhile cause he would be assisting. He had been torn. Posing for the calendar irked him beyond belief but he couldn't them down. Building a facility in each capital city to assist those foster-children who had turned eighteen and were aging out of the system was so needed and such a huge task. Although it went against his better judgement to bring attention to himself, he'd decided that he needed to put the charity first. He would deal with repercussions, if any arose, later.

'How noble of you to go ahead, then.' Laine rolled her eyes, unaware of his knowledge and belief in the charity. She was not impressed. She took both her work and the cause seriously and she was annoyed with his apparent lack of respect towards her and the project. This charity meant the world to her. She would give, and do, whatever she could to help make a difference to the lives of foster-children. Someone had to.

It was tough being in foster-care sometimes but it was even tougher when the stay came to an end. Laine knew that firsthand. She wanted to provide assistance for the children before the system scarred them and also to assist those transitioning into adulthood. She had been involved with the charity for a number of years, and each year she took on a greater workload. Some days when the loneliness of the life she had chosen was almost untenable, she thought of all the foster-children enduring a swinging-door childhood and knew there had to be a way to improve their lives. Any assistance she could provide from her connections and her work she would give without reservation.

Carefully, and in silence, she continued to pack away her equipment, cleaning the front and rear elements of her lenses before storing them. She was fastidious about the tools of her trade and valued everything she owned. She used the best, she could afford it, but it hadn't always been that way and having scrimped and saved when starting out for even the basic photographic equipment ensured she never took any of her belongings for granted now.

'I might have to do this shoot but I sure as hell don't

have to climb up a ladder again. In fact, I'm calling the shots tomorrow. My way or *no* way,' Pierce said, not masking his disdain for the entire situation.

Laine looked at the man who would be her subject for the next two days and knew it could easily become one of the most frustrating and difficult assignments of her almost ten year career. Frustrating because of the subject, difficult because of the location. Dr Pierce Beaumont was ridiculously uncooperative and Uralla held memories she wanted to forget.

When she'd left the small town, almost three hundred miles north of Sydney, all those years before, she had never expected to return. A part of her past, it bore no relevance to the life she had forged in New York. Laine knew she had never been happier than when she'd lived in Uralla but she also knew she wasn't that girl any more and she could never fit into this town again.

She was a citizen of the world, a woman for whom her career was her entire life. There was no room and no need for anyone else in it—and particularly not the people of this town. They were warm and welcoming but she didn't want that level of sentiment in her life. It didn't fit with her any more. Those years living in a small town had allowed her to finally understand what it felt like to be a part of a family. Someone had actually cared how she'd felt and had wanted her to be safe and protected. For the very first time she had stopped feeling abandoned. She had stopped expecting that all promises would eventually be broken.

The perfect picture she'd painted of a life with one loving family—a life she had only dreamt of when she'd constantly moved homes, meeting new foster-families and being bullied by foster-siblings—had actually come true. It had been a home where she'd learned the true meaning of unconditional love, and one that had provided the answer to the question she had asked all her life: *Where did she belong?* It was right there.

But after four wonderful years it had all come to a terrible, tragic end. Her adoptive parents had died in a car accident. They were gone, and never coming back— and she had been alone once again.

So Laine had used the scars to give her strength. She'd turned her back on the security of the small town and chosen a new life, far away from Uralla. It had taken years to finally become successful but she'd known she could do it. Eventually, her determination to take control of her life, to make the most of every day and to rely on absolutely no one had driven her to the top.

Travelling the world, working with models and managing their demands, and those of the clients, at fashion shoots and waking up in a different hotel every day had finally become way of life for Laine. It was a mad schedule but being frantically busy allowed her to keep her thoughts of the past at bay. There were lonely times but it was the price she paid for the life she led and she never complained. Even the demands of models didn't unnerve her. They all had a job to do and at the end of the assignment they all had great shots in their portfolios. If they played the thorny card, Laine was at a level in her career when she could refuse to work with them again, and generally bad attitudes meant their careers were short-lived.

Laine loved what she did. It was that simple. She was a well-respected photographer and she never needed to look for work. Her name was synonymous with work in high-end magazines representing the finest fashion houses and most expensive jewellery lines, and recently she had completed an assignment on the Italian Riviera for an iconic sports-car company. Her portfolio was eclectic, with the most beautiful, timeless and cutting-edge photographs of any living photographer.

She had worked hard for everything she had achieved and no doctor from New South Wales with little or no knowledge of her profession was going to try and tell her what to do.

She was not little Melanie Phillips of Uralla. That young girl no longer existed. She was Laine Phillips, international photographer. She wasn't about to be pushed around by any man, however handsome or crucial to her shoot.

'So you're styling the shoot tomorrow? Interesting premise.' Laine took a deep breath and sat down cross-legged near the last of the bags she was packing. There was absolutely no way he would be making any decisions about tomorrow, other than his choice of cologne. She would dictate everything else about the shoot. It was her name and reputation on these photographs and that meant she was the one in control. Just as she had been about everything in her life for the last twelve years. No one took control from her hands. *Ever.*

'If you think you can waltz into our town and lay down the law, you can think again.' Pierce was not impressed with her desire to order him about. He wouldn't tolerate it and he could make her stay increasingly difficult if she kept it up. She could take her arrogant, big-city outlook and hop straight back on a plane. 'Don't bring your condescending attitude here. I'm doing you a favour.'

'Me a favour? You're helping a charity, not me personally. And not doing a lot except taking off your clothes. Hardly a huge ask. So contrary to your suggestion about running things tomorrow I have bad news for you. The shoot will be done *Laine's way*.'

Pierce eyed the stunning brunette who had just given him a serving. She certainly wasn't a shrinking violet. She was a tiny dictator of sorts. A very beautiful dictator. He wondered for a moment why she wasn't on the other side of the camera. Her flawless figure was evident in a tight white singlet top and faded blue jeans. She was a natural beauty with little, if any, make-up, yet she didn't seem to fuss about her appearance. But he needed to forget how attractive she was and remember that she was telling him what to do—and he didn't take kindly to that.

'I can sit on a tractor on the McKenzies' farm. No great planning needed. Country doctor, on a farm, on a tractor. Shoot done. Photo taken. *It's a wrap*—isn't that what they say?'

Laine rolled her eyes. She couldn't believe how little he valued or understood her craft. In his eyes, her livelihood was quickly and simply reduced to plonking a doctor on a tractor and taking a snap.

'Perhaps you could just take a selfie with your phone and send it to me?' Laine was not about to try and explain the process she undertook in planning and delivering a quality shoot to a man who had no idea. She continued zipping up the last of her bags.

'I still don't agree with the calendar idea,' he remarked, choosing to ignore her sarcasm.

'It's a proven formula,' she replied matter-of-factly.

'Eligible shirtless men, with a bit of tweaking, become every woman's fantasy.'

'Tweaking?' he asked, with a frown knitting his dark brows. 'You are on a roll, aren't you? Do you insult all of your subjects so matter-of-factly?'

Laine stopped what she was doing for a moment and looking at Pierce with a stoic expression replied, 'It wasn't an insult. It's a fact. I edit photos to bring out the best and hide the flaws. Photography is often pure fantasy. I make the subject irresistible. Whether it's a string of pearls, a leather handbag or an automobile that only two per cent of the population could actually afford to buy. I make it the most desirable possession. Something the consumer cannot live without. I make it shinier than it really is, more beautiful than it might be and in doing so turn it into the stuff of dreams.'

'So it's all smoke and mirrors?' Pierce remarked. 'No real shots for you. Nothing of any depth. Doesn't really surprise me. It's just about selling a product, full stop.'

'And what gives you the right to say that? You know nothing about me,' she retorted, getting back to her feet and facing him. 'I love my gritty real shots, like photographing older people. I don't remove a single line or make any changes. The character in faces that have seen hardship and joy in equal amounts are priceless. But if I'm contracted to make a product sell, then I will tweak until I can't tweak any more!'

Laine knew well enough that none of Pierce's shots would need any editing on her behalf. He had a kind of refined magnetism that would stir any female and she wouldn't tamper with *that*.

The last hour in Pierce's presence had been professionally frustrating but that was the least of her problems. There was something about this man and this situation that was making Laine feel ill at ease. Whether it was Pierce's very real and very natural sensuality or just being back in Uralla wasn't clear to her, but something was making her feel uncomfortable.

She was accustomed to models and their ability to turn it on and turn it off, but Pierce didn't seem to have a switch. He was genuinely this sexy, twenty-four seven. It was innate and palpable and he had an inner strength that shone though. And for some inexplicable reason he was unnerving her.

'Were you being difficult for the sake of it or was it another reason why you didn't want to take the step up the ladder?' she asked, trying to bring the conversation back to business. 'You really did seem to overreact to my request.'

'I told you that I didn't want to be involved. Let's leave it at that. You won't convince me that there's not a better or easier way to raise funds to support your charity.'

Laine turned away again and wound up the cords draped across the floor. She suspected there was more to his reticence in taking that step than just arrogance but she thought better of pursuing the matter. She just wanted to finish the shoot on time and get away from him. With the cords packed up, she closed her laptop, slipped it into her backpack and turned towards him.

'They did their market research and decided on a calendar. It worked for the firemen last year so the charity chose twelve of Australia's most eligible general practitioners. And you, Dr Beaumont, have the dubious honour of being the last for the year. You're Dr December,' she announced as she zipped up the last of her bags.

'Call me Pierce, Dr Beaumont is way too formal and correct me if I'm wrong, as I'm sure you will, but I can't see anything around here that looks at all festive.' Pierce rubbed his chin and added dryly, 'What about I remove what's left of my clothing and you strategically place a Christmas tree in front of me?'

Pierce would never normally have spoken this way to a woman he barely knew. His behaviour was always beyond reproach. *Always*. But with his feet securely on the ground and his anger subsiding, Laine's behaviour was bringing out a different, irreverent side of him and he suspected with her New York attitude Laine could take it. And give it back. She clearly wasn't the shy type.

'Strategically positioned Christmas tree?' she muttered as she returned her gaze to him. Suddenly her heart began to race. She had to push the visual from her mind. He was leaning on the desk with his arms folded across the ripples of his tanned chest. She had captured photos of some incredibly good-looking men over the last three weeks, but he was clearly the most handsome. Hands down. She swallowed and tried to think of him as just another subject but he was different from the other doctors. They had been helpful and a little flattered to be asked and two had even very politely invited her out to dinner, which she had equally politely refused, but Pierce Beaumont had an attitude that both annoyed and intrigued her.

She wasn't sure that he knew just how good looking he was, but she suspected he knew women would not run away from his advances. He wasn't overly close but there was electricity in the air she had to cut. It made her feel uncomfortable that he was stirring up feelings she didn't want to feel. She had another two days' shooting with him and she couldn't let him get under her skin.

Laine hated to admit it but the sight of his toned body so close to her did make her breathing a little shallow. She bit her lip. This was crazy. She had filmed ludicrously handsome male models for an underwear shoot in a New York subway a month ago and they had left her cold. It had always been a job. But now this country doctor with his defiance and an aversion to ladders was making her feel very self-conscious.

She had to push him away. She preferred being alone. No one to depend on. No one who could leave and make her feel as if her heart had broken in two, wondering whether she could go on. No, Laine Phillips was alone in this world and she liked it that way.

'Perhaps mistletoe would suffice,' she replied, as she scooped up her bag and walked towards the door.

Pierce smirked at her remark. He was right, she could dish it up, and do it well. Perhaps another couple of days with this gorgeous brunette, despite the circumstances, would be less traumatic than he imagined. She had spirit. He crossed the room, picked up the heavier bag containing the grip and lighting equipment and walked to the door with it. Reaching for the handle, he opened the door for Laine with his free hand.

'Mistletoe will definitely *not* suffice,' he said as she squeezed past him, the narrowness of the doorway causing her bare shoulder to inadvertently brush lightly across his chest. 'Not even close.'

CHAPTER TWO

LAINE WAS AMUSED and a little taken aback by Pierce's comment. This country doctor definitely had an edge to him. He was actually a little more *city* than she had first imagined. She smiled to herself then decided to delete the mental image that had crept into her mind. Edge or no edge, this trip to Uralla needed to stay professional. The thought of Pierce as anything more than a photo shoot couldn't happen. Not even a fling. Her flings were very separate from her work.

Gossip spread quickly in the circles in which she travelled and she wasn't about to become the photographer who overstepped the mark and fell into bed with her models. No matter how tempting it could be at times. It risked a shift in power. It also complicated life and she had never allowed herself to become fodder for rumours. It was one of her rules.

Along with another, which prevented her flings developing into relationships. Her heart was safely tucked away behind a stone wall that was carved with her rules. Her own invisible armour, it kept her safe from ever becoming attached to another person. From ever needing someone, only to find they had gone. From ever feeling secure, only to find she was alone again.

Laine Phillips was a one-woman show. And nothing would ever change that. Definitely not a three-day stop-over in Uralla.

'You can put your shirt on now,' she told him, without looking again at his stunning physique. 'The shoot is over.'

Her professional demeanour was in full throttle now, he thought. Perhaps it had been his remark about the mistletoe, he mused. His intention had been to lighten the mood, but clearly that wasn't about to happen in the near future. She had shut him down and any light-hearted banter was over. Apparently Laine Phillips was all business.

Drawing breath, he looked at her very pretty face. It was devoid of emotion. He wondered what her story was—what made this very attractive woman so defensive. So aloof and untouchable. Her walls were so high that Pierce wondered if it was more than big-city conceit. This seemed more personal.

Laine Phillips seemed to be a gorgeous island that perhaps no one had ever discovered.

He found it odd that he was making sweeping statements in his own head about a woman he barely knew. He had never summed up a woman so quickly. He had never *wanted* to before. But she was such an enigma.

'So shall I meet you at the McKenzies' property tomorrow morning around four-thirty?'

'Four-thirty in the morning?' he questioned her, as he did up the last of his shirt buttons. 'Are we milking the cows?'

Her eyes smiled. She didn't give her mouth permission to do the same. 'It's the perfect lighting then. Nothing to do with cows. I want to capture you in the wide-open paddock just as the sun rises, with a single eucalyptus tree on the horizon. Single man, single tree. Blatant symbolism.'

'Single eucalyptus tree?' he asked with a quizzical frown dividing his dark brows. 'Have you actually seen the McKenzies' property or are you just hoping to find a backdrop like that?'

Laine shifted the heavy bag a little on her shoulder. She didn't want to admit she knew the property like the back of her hand. That she had spent time there when she'd been growing up. She had hoped to avoid questions like this but realised that it was nearly impossible. When she had discovered that Dr Pierce Beaumont, her final shoot in the calendar, was the resident general practitioner in Uralla she had been filled with dread. When the bus had pulled out of the town all those years ago, its final destination Sydney, she had begun to barricade her emotions—one brick at a time. Each signpost she had passed had laid another piece of rock around her heart.

For a few years Sydney had become her home and then New York. She chose cities that prevented her from forming lasting relationships. Cities as cold and detached as the person she needed to become. She wasn't strong enough to remain in a town as kind as Uralla. She didn't have any more tears, or anything left inside to save her again. There could never be another heartache, for the next one would most definitely be the end of her. So Melanie Phillips had taken matters into her own hands. She had changed her name just enough to feel like a different person and she'd moved on, successfully burying herself in a busy and demanding life. A life without love and all the risks and sadness it brought.

When she had agreed to the calendar assignment, Laine had had no inkling that she would be spending time in this familiar little town in country New South Wales. She'd assumed it would be capital cities or large beachside towns. Not a town so small it didn't really factor into most people's knowledge of Australian geography. It was as pretty as a picture but famous for nothing more than being not too far from the centre of country music in Australia and for having a major highway as a main street. It was a town where you could leave your front door unlocked and know nothing would be taken because the locals were either family or friends.

She had once loved living there and now she assumed Pierce felt the same.

'I was out at the McKenzies' this morning. I drove there to check the setting was suitable after my plane touched down in Armidale.'

Pierce's curiosity was further heightened but he said nothing, keeping his thoughts to himself as he watched her nervously shift her stance. He had no right to question her or ask more about her than she was willing to offer. He was a private person. His past was off limits so why should hers be any different?

His life had effectively started when he'd come to Uralla two years before. He had never spoken about his past or his family, except to say that his aunt had been given custody of him after his parents had passed away when he was a child. The circle of people his father and mother had once called friends had never tried to make contact after the tragedy so they hadn't factored into his thoughts as he'd grown older. When the parties on his parents' yacht had ceased, so had their friends' interest in Pierce.

However, their children had sought him out years later, when he'd been a young adult. At first he'd thought they'd actually cared about their friendship with him, but that belief had been short-lived when it had become clear these long-lost friends had only needed him to pay their tabs. It hadn't taken long for Pierce to realise that all they really valued was his family money—especially the women. All eager to snare a wealthy husband, they never tried to hide their love of the luxury lifestyle they assumed he would lavish on them if they were to become his wife.

Pierce wanted none of it. He wanted what his parents had never had. *Real* friends. The type that didn't care if your car was twenty years old and gave you a place to sleep if you needed it. Although he would never need to be given a helping hand with regard to money—he was indisputably one of the richest young men in Australia. His wealth, generated from his father's mining and real estate interests, was handled by his business manager in Sydney.

And so, one day, when he'd realised he wanted more from his life, Pierce had simply disappeared from high society and moved to a town he had heard about during medical school. A town that he hoped he would be happy to call home.

The townsfolk never asked more than he was willing to give, they never pried into his past, and he was happy with that arrangement. Everything he'd done after driving down the New England Highway and into Uralla was on the table. Anything before that was not discussed. The circus that had been his life had dissipated just as he had hoped. His new life was too quiet and uneventful to create any interest in the media—in fact, many thought that his inheritance was all gone, the proceeds lost to bad investments.

Out of the eyes of the press, Pierce quietly directed the accountant to make donations in the company name to deserving causes. A silent philanthropist, he never used any of the money in his personal life. And he wouldn't want it any other way. He knew who his friends were and without the family money there would be fewer enemies. Keeping his past to himself was working quite nicely.

Perhaps Laine had her reasons too. Clearly her accent was Australian, albeit with an international flavour, and he knew she was based in New York. He had just assumed she would have grown up in another big city like Sydney. But somehow she knew her way around Uralla.

'I know the town, I spent some time here eons ago,' Laine told him. She didn't want to get into it so kept the explanation brief. 'But it's immaterial. I just need you there at four-thirty and then in the late afternoon I thought we'd head over to Saumarez Homestead. They have a barn with a spectacular panoramic view. I would like to capture you in the doorway just as the sun sets.'

'Lighting, right?'

'Yes, lighting and amazing scenery. New England is a stunning part of Australia and I want to do it justice,' she said, then added, 'Besides, the early morning shoot will allow you to see patients during the day and then we can head out again around five in the afternoon. Minimal disruption to your day and daylight saving will add value to mine, giving me sufficient time to set up my equipment and still catch the sunset.'

'Yes, my patients,' Pierce remarked. He felt slightly guilty that being so close to this woman had made him almost forget the day ahead. No woman had ever made such an impression in such a short space of time. She was a conundrum. He wanted to know more about her but he didn't feel he had the right to ask too many questions. It was against his view of life, his belief in respecting privacy and boundaries. Suddenly those values began slipping as the desire to know everything he could about this woman began to grow. Her confidence was evident but it was not grandiose. She seemed so focused and serious. Almost a little too serious.

'You really do have a feel for this town. I'm assuming it wasn't a fleeting visit or, if it was, this sleepy enclave made an impression on you.' He wasn't able to mask his interest any longer—plus, there was also the chance she might open up just a little.

Laine took a deep breath. The town had left more than an impression. It had been the best and worst. The happiest and saddest. It had been her life and then it had ended. Laine knew she had to put the past behind her. She had an assignment to complete and a very different life waiting for her in New York and wherever in the world she was called to work next. Uralla had to remain business—sentiment didn't pay dividends for her any more.

'I will not intrude on any more of your time than I have to over the next couple of days, I promise,' she replied, ignoring his comment. 'But now I need to get these bags to my car and head back to my hotel. I have calls to make and emails to attend to this evening.'

'Sure. Let me take one of those.' Pierce accepted Laine's right to pass on answering him and reached for one of her bags, walking to the back door of the practice. It was an old red-brick house that had been converted into three consulting rooms, an office and a small surgery for minor medical procedures. The large backyard—complete with a clothesline on a slight Tower of Pisa lean and a wire chicken coop housing four large laying hens—had been retained, with patient parking relegated to the street. It was picture-perfect country rustic.

Looking at her surroundings, Laine realised she had almost forgotten the relaxed feel of the country. Her designer, sparsely decorated apartment on the fourth floor of a Manhattan apartment building had none of that ambience. And it was of her choosing. Nothing she didn't need and nothing she would miss when she was away. Streamlined and minimalist.

Focused on keeping childhood memories at bay, she followed Pierce through the yard and out of the back gate to where a large silver four-wheel-drive hire car was parked on the side of the road under the shade of a huge leafy tree. She opened the rear door and placed the equipment inside.

'I'm staying at the Bushranger Inn down the street. I can come past and collect you in the morning or meet you there,' she remarked casually as she closed the heavy door on her belongings. Trying to do the same to her thoughts, she made her way to the driver's side. It was the opposite side from the left-hand drive she was accustomed to but, as a New Yorker who mainly took cabs around the city, she found adjusting wasn't that difficult.

'What about I pick you up and I drive us there?' he returned.

'I'm perfectly capable of driving both of us,' she retorted, before she closed the door, turned on the engine and dropped the electric window. 'But since you don't want me to drive you, I'll meet you there.' Without another word, she put the car into gear and headed off in the direction of her hotel only half a mile down the road, leaving Pierce open-mouthed on the side of the road. Her exit was abrupt, to say the least.

Pierce had not meant to offend her. He had been trying to make up for his less-than-gracious attitude during the shoot with his offer. He quickly realised that what he had thought a gallant act had been something that she'd perceived as insulting, perhaps chauvinistic. He wasn't entirely sure. Clearly he couldn't win. She had driven off so hurriedly it had been as if she couldn't wait to get away from him.

'What the hell was that about?' he muttered as he walked inside. He was still shaking his head in frustration as he closed the back door and headed to the kitchen. Despite his best intentions to forget Laine, and her borderline rudeness, as he made his first coffee of the day the New York photographer had his full attention.

'Good morning, dearie. Who was that motoring off at lightning speed down the road?' came a voice behind him.

Pierce knew it was his receptionist Tracy, a retired nurse and wife of the former practice owner. Tracy worked three days a week, job-sharing with another local nurse.

'Morning Trace,' he replied, turning around with

his coffee. 'The racing-car driver you just missed was the New York photographer in town to shoot the charity calendar.'

'Was she in a hurry or did you two have words? You seem a little stressed.'

'You might say that,' he said, then, noticing her face quickly develop a frown, he added, 'I thought I was being a gentleman, but somehow I still managed to offend her.'

'You know, if I'm to marry you off, young man you have to be nice to these young ladies. She was young, wasn't she?'

'Yes, young and very beautiful.'

Tracy watched his face curiously. She hadn't seen him look that way since she'd met him. The woman must be quite something for him to have this reaction.

'Then you need to find a way to see her again.' With that she put her lunch in the refrigerator and headed to the waiting room. Tracy knew that fewer words with Pierce always had a better response.

Pierce had already decided that was exactly what he would do after he finished the day. Thinking about how he could arrange it, he picked up his coffee, took a sip from the steaming cup and headed to his office to switch on his computer and check through the patient roster for the morning.

When Pierce had joined the practice two years previously, all the patient records had been hard-copy files with coloured coded spines. It had taken some convincing for the hesitant older partner, Dr Majors, to see the value in moving everything onto what Pierce had touted as a more efficient electronic system. It had meant hiring another administration person to transfer the patient records into the new format but after a sound argument from Pierce, Dr Majors had accepted a small trial. Once the older practitioner had seen the benefit of the system, he'd agreed that the new technology was needed across the entire practice and the surgery had made a much-needed move into the twenty-first century.

A few minutes later he stood in the doorway of the waiting room. 'Carla Hollis, can you please come in?' Stepping back, he let the young woman steer her pram into his consulting room, then closed the door and crossed back to his desk.

'So how is little James today?' he asked as Carla lifted her baby from the pram. 'I see you've brought him in for his four-month immunisation.'

'I have, but I'm not sure, Dr Armstrong, he doesn't seem well today,' she replied, nursing the infant on her lap. His quickly wriggled his feet free of the blue cotton blanket.

Pierce wheeled his chair closer to the pair. 'In what way do you mean unwell? Can you be more specific?'

'He's had a slight runny nose for a few days now. It turned into a cough three days ago but last night I was up so often that I brought him into bed with us. He kept us awake for hours then finally stopped coughing about three in the morning,' she said, pulling her long blonde plait free of his chubby fingers. 'He still has an appetite and he's been breastfeeding so maybe there's nothing to worry about.'

Pierce took some disposable gloves from the dispenser on his desk. He slipped them on before he carefully unwrapped the little boy from his soft blue cocoon, lifted up his singlet and, in turn, placed the stethoscope on his chest then his back. Pierce pulled the clothing down again and placed a thermometer under his arm, holding it there for a few moments.

'Any persistent cough is a concern in an infant and James also has a slight fever,' he replied, after checking the reading. 'It's difficult to tell the difference between whooping cough and another respiratory infection, but I'd prefer to err on the side of caution. I'll take a swab of his nose to test for the Bordetella pertussis bacterium, which indicates whooping cough, but I won't wait for the results before we start antibiotics. The test can take time and it can quickly become serious in babies as young as James.'

'But didn't he have a shot for that when he was two months old?'

'Yes, he did,' Pierce responded as he stood, crossed to the consulting room trolley and collected what he needed to take a swab and returned to the mother and child. 'That was the first of the three immunisations he requires. One at two months, the next at four months and again at six months. Unfortunately, until he has completed all three he can still contract whooping cough.' Pierce gently held the infant's head steady, took a sample from his nose and placed it into a sterile lab container.

'But he will be all right, won't he?'

'I have no reason to think otherwise,' Pierce answered as he discarded his gloves, sat back down at his desk and began completing the online patient records. 'Has James been around anyone with a persistent cough?'

'We had family visit from Tamworth on the weekend and my nieces were coughing all night. I kept James away from them but my sister insisted on holding him,'

Carla replied, as she lifted the child up and gently patted his back.

'If James does have whooping cough, it's very contagious. He may have contracted it from direct contact with someone infected with the bacterium—perhaps your sister—or by simply breathing the air within six feet of someone infected with the germs. The bacteria usually enter the nose or throat. We won't know for sure until the test result comes back but until then please keep his fluids up. We don't want to risk dehydration,' Pierce said, as he pulled the script request from the printer and handed it to Carla.

'If he becomes tired from coughing and can't take a full feed, you will need to give him small regular feeds. Bring his bassinette into your room for the next few nights and keep an eye on him until the coughing has completely gone. Babies can develop apnoea as a complication of whooping cough, which means he may stop breathing for short periods.'

Suddenly the baby began a bout of coughing. It escalated quickly to a point where he was struggling for breath. Pierce immediately lifted him from his mother's arms and supported him in an upright position to make breathing easier. The cough was severe and Pierce immediately knew that James had been infected for longer than his mother suspected and was past home care with antibiotics.

'That's how he coughed all last night,' Carla gasped, and her eyes widened with concern at the infant's condition.

'It could be bronchiolitis or whooping cough but either way I want to transfer him to New England District hospital immediately. They are better equipped to help him through the illness. Antibiotics will need to be administered, as I first told you, but James needs to have oxygen delivered through a tiny mask during these coughing episodes.'

He stepped outside his consulting room and into the waiting area. 'Tracy, can you call for an ambulance, please? Relay that it is not an emergency but we need a monitored transfer to New England District. Carla can't drive and attend to James at the same time.'

Stepping back into the room where Carla sat, chewing her lip nervously, Pierce continued, 'James will need to spend a while in hospital, but I want you to have this in case you need me.' He handed her a card with his twenty-four-hour paging number. 'And don't hesitate to call if you have any concerns. One more thing, if it is confirmed that James has whooping cough, then the chances are high you will both will have contracted it, too. So if you get *any* sign of a cough, immediately begin antibiotics. If you don't, it may take six to ten weeks to subside and nothing will make the recovery quicker once you pass the initial two-week period. Please call your sister too and get her off to her family GP in Tamworth as soon as possible.'

'My husband was coughing last night too, so I'll get him onto the antibiotics tonight. Should I give him a cough suppressant so he can sleep?' Carla asked, as she gently placed the now quiet baby back into his pram to await the ambulance.

'I don't recommend it. I'd prefer to let him cough. It's what the body naturally does when it needs to clear the lungs of mucus and I prefer not to suppress that reaction.'

Carla stood up and took the new script that Pierce

held out to her. 'I'll give the hospital a call later and speak to the paediatrician about the treatment plan for James.' With that he wheeled the pram through the waiting room and directed Carla into the spare consulting room. 'The ambulance should be here quite soon but until then you can wait here comfortably.'

Pierce explained to Tracy his reasoning for keeping Carla separate from the waiting patients. If he was correct with his diagnosis of James, he suspected that over the next few days there would be a few more of their family and friends appearing with whooping cough but at least keeping Carla isolated until the ambulance arrived might help those in the surgery that morning.

Laine turned into the narrow driveway of her motel, past Reception and continued driving down to her room. She pulled up at the front of the Ned Kelly room, her cosy home for the three-night stay. She had checked in a few hours earlier. She unpacked her equipment from the car and carefully stacked it up against the wall inside her room. It didn't take too long before the car was empty and her room looked like a photographic warehouse.

Tossing her sunglasses and keys on the bed, she crossed to the window and pulled it open to enjoy the fresh air. It felt so good to fill her lungs. It was a welcome change to the hotels where she routinely stayed. Her usual accommodation was elegant and never less than five star, but there was also never a window to be opened and always an abundance of pollution in most major cities when she stepped outside.

Laine stood motionless, looking out across the open paddock, and thought back to when she'd lived in the town. It had been over a decade ago but nothing much appeared to have changed.

Part of her wanted to take a walk around her old town. To feel like she belonged, the way it had been all those years ago. Now she was a stranger in her home town. But she didn't want to come face to face with the people who had been like her extended family when she'd been growing up—there was still the chance they might recognise her. It had been twelve long years and she certainly wasn't the Melanie they would remember.

Quite apart from her new name, she had grown out her trademark super-short pixie cut, the chubbiness of her baby face even as a teenager had been replaced by an elongated profile and her braces were long gone. The awkward teen with the tomboy dress sense, who would milk the cows, help to plant the crops, shoo away the crows and look forward to a twenty-minute car trip into Armidale as if there were no bigger treat possible, no longer existed. She had left that life far behind. She didn't belong in this town any more.

Laine walked away from the window with her heart suddenly, and unexpectedly, aching for her past. And even more for what had been taken from her. She kicked off her designer espadrilles and lay back on the bed, looking up at the ceiling. Her eyes closed and her mind slipped back to a happy time. A time when she'd felt loved and protected and wanted. Turning on her side, she felt a tear slip from her eye and roll down her cheek. It had been many years since she had stopped and yearned for that time in her life.

She wiped the tear away with the back of her hand, and silently berated herself for being swept up in emotions after only a few hours of being in the town. It was silly. Melancholy musings had no place in her life. She was an independent woman with no ties, just the way she liked it. *The way it needed to be*, she told herself, before she drifted off for a much-needed nap. The frantic six-week schedule she had given herself hadn't factored in any down time between shoots and flights and finally it had caught up with her.

Hours later she was woken from her slumber by a knock at the door.

Laine sat upright, staring at the wooden door, with no clue as to who would be on the other side. Waking with memories still so close to the surface, it quickly took Laine back to a time when she would run from a knock at the door. When she had felt sure someone was coming to take her away from the loving home she had found. Earlier in her childhood, the knock had signalled that the authorities had been called and a decision made to move her to the next placement. She became numb and often didn't care as she'd been leaving a less-than-pleasant situation, but all that had changed when she'd come to live with the Phillips family and found a place she'd truly wanted to call home. Then the knock would send her scurrying to hide so that they couldn't find her and rip her away from a place where she felt safe. Over time, with help from her new parents, she'd learnt that a knock did not signal something ominous. It merely meant visitors were arriving and she learnt to embrace the sound.

Then there was Manhattan, where no one knocked on her door unexpectedly. They had to call from the lobby and she or the concierge had to let them up. Laine liked it that way.

She quickly looked around the clean motel room. The housekeeping was done. There was no reason for anyone to be calling on her. No one knew she was in town. The arrangement to use the McKenzie property had been done by a third party so they had no knowledge she was in town.

'Laine, it's Pierce,' came the deep voice from the other side of the door. She could hear him clearly. There was no other noise. No sounds of taxi horns or police sirens or people partying in the room above. For a brief moment Laine found comfort in the silence. It was so peaceful until the knocking started again.

'I've finished up for the day and thought we might grab a bite to eat,' he suggested tentatively through the still-closed door. 'If you're up to it.'

Laine was hungry but the thought of spending more time than absolutely necessary with Pierce was unsettling. He was an incredibly attractive man with charisma and home-grown charm and she was feeling slightly vulnerable, being back in this town. It was as if the warm memories of her past were trying to thaw her now cold outlook on life. She didn't like the feeling at all. She didn't like having her resolve questioned.

Pretending to be asleep wasn't as option as it was only seven o'clock. So, grudgingly, she climbed from the bed and made her way barefoot to the door.

'About dinner, I'm not sure,' she began as she opened the door. Pierce was leaning against the wall, dressed in jeans, one dusty boot having caught the lip of a red brick. His grey checked shirt was unbuttoned at the neck, hiding the perfectly toned chest she'd already been privy to. He was handsome in any light but it wasn't an arrogant or cocky assurance he had. It was the confidence a man had when he knew himself. One who wasn't searching for anything. One who had found what he was looking for. She wondered for a moment if Pierce had found himself in Uralla or had he arrived already content?

He dropped his booted foot to the ground and turned to face her. 'I'm heading to the top pub for a quick meal and I thought you might like to join me.'

His smile was perfect but more than that it was genuine. Laine was accustomed to the perfect smile that a model managed to show on cue but with no actual meaning behind it. Her stomach fluttered. Another feeling she was not expecting or enjoying. Her mind told her to feign a headache and slam the door but the clear country evening with a hint of his cologne convinced her heart to accept his invitation.

'I guess that would be okay.'

She was surprised by her own reaction. She was not spontaneous like this. She always weighed up all the options and then, after careful consideration through a jaded lens, she chose the one that would best fit her schedule. On the way to retrieve her purse from her backpack near the window, Laine heard alarm bells ringing in her head. They were as clear as every other sound she had heard since she had arrived in the quiet little town that morning, but they were in her own mind and her heart quickly shut them down as she slipped her espadrilles back on.

Something was driving her to spend time with the man at her door. And her cold New York reasoning was losing this battle. Her head was in a spin and she was going with it, even if it was against her usual calculated judgement.

'I think this will go well,' he remarked, as she closed the door to her room. 'Neither of us has to drive as it's walking distance so I can't offend you again.'

Laine allowed her mouth to curve into a smile as they made their way up the bitumen driveway to the main road.

'So they still call them the *top* pub and the *bottom* pub?'

'Yes, not sure why really but no one ever says meet you at the Coachwood and Cedar or the Thunderbolt, it's just the top or bottom pub.'

Laine smiled again at the way nothing had changed, but it was a bittersweet smile as they walked past the bottom pub and spied numerous patrons outside, enjoying a beer and a chat in the balmy evening breeze. She reminded herself she would only be in town for a few days and that after that her life would return to the one she knew. The life she had grown accustomed to. A life on her own on the other side of the world. And with any luck no one would recognise her tonight or any time over the next few days.

They meandered their way to their choice of venue for the evening, only a block away. It was a small town but the locals still managed to support two hotels and a number of cafés and restaurants.

Pierce held the door open and they stepped inside. It was hive of activity. It was mid-week and still busy. There was a drone of patrons' happy chatter and clinking of glasses as they walked through the front bar towards the dining section.

'G'day, Doc,' came a gruff voice just before they reached the dining area, followed by a hearty pat on Pierce's back. 'Who's the pretty lady? Even blind as a bat without my glasses I can see she's beautiful. And just to let you know, I'll be disappointed if you tell me she's your sister.'

Laine saw the older man smiling in her direction. She recognised him immediately but realised he didn't have the same recollection. Her stomach dropped. It was Jim Patterson, her father's best friend. He had more silver in his still thick wavy hair and his face was a little more lined but the twinkle in his blue eyes hadn't changed at all. For thirty years, the pair would relax over a cold beer on a Sunday afternoon on the back veranda. Jim was older than her father by quite a few years but they had struck up a friendship while working on the land as jackeroos when Arthur had just left school and Jim had been in his late twenties. Laine had gone to school with two of his four sons. She looked at Jim's face and for a moment she thought he might have remembered but she could see there was nothing. She was relieved that his vision was challenged without his glasses.

'Jim,' Pierce said, stepping back to let the old man closer to Laine. 'This is Laine. She's a photographer from New York.'

'New York, hey?' He laughed. 'Well, I'm pleased to meet you but old Uralla is a long way from your neck of the woods, young lady. What brings you from the Big Apple to our little town?'

'An assignment actually,' she replied, meeting the older man's handshake. 'I'm shooting a charity calendar to aid FCTP. Foster Children's Transition Programme. Pierce is my final subject.'

The old man nudged Pierce in the ribs and laughed again. 'So, you're a pin-up now? Uralla's own poster boy. Well, that's a hoot.' Then he turned his attention back to Laine. 'You're not shooting him in his boxers, though, are you, love? That wouldn't be something I'd want on the wall, but then again maybe the ladies would like it.'

Laine smiled at Jim and remembered he always had a great sense of humour. When he lost Claire he was beside himself with grief but the townsfolk lifted his spirits and made sure he was never alone. They cooked meals, helped him take care of his sons as the youngest was only eight, and they carried him through the sadness to a better place. And clearly he had stayed there and was back to his old self.

'Not his boxers. He's in jeans but that's about it.' Laine smirked as she watched Pierce's face fall.

'Enough of that,' he announced, changing the subject. 'I'll let you go, Jim, so we can get a table.' Turning his full attention to Laine, he added, 'Maybe we can talk about your history with Uralla? "Eons ago" was the term you used. I was hoping over a glass of wine you might elaborate on that just a little.' Pierce pulled out a chair for Laine.

Laine suddenly felt a cold shiver run over her before a large lump formed in her throat. Accepting the dinner invitation had been a huge mistake. She had been fooling herself to think she could enjoy dinner with Pierce and not have to talk about herself and her connection to the town. She didn't talk about herself. Not ever. Her private life was a closed book and she intended to keep it that way. She thought he had accepted that but apparently not. The night had to end. Now.

'I'm sorry, Pierce, I completely forgot there's a call I need to make to one of my editors in the US. I'll be crucified if I don't do it,' she lied, moving away from the chair and Pierce. 'You eat and if I finish quickly, I'll come back and join you,' she lied again, before she made her way back through the crowded front bar. Laine had no intention of returning for a dinner she anticipated would spiral into the Spanish Inquisition.

With that, she rushed out of the top pub, leaving Pierce alone, and made her way down the street. Anxiously she looked back over her shoulder once or twice and when she felt confident that Pierce was not following her, she ran into the bottom pub and sat down at the furthest table from the door. Her stomach was feeling empty from hunger and churning with nerves. She wasn't sure if the motel restaurant would be open, so she decided to grab a quick meal at the pub then head back to her room.

Dinner with Pierce would have been impossible. She had been naïve to accept the invitation and not expect that it would mean bringing up the past. Losing her family in Uralla gave her more heartache than she'd thought possible for one person to bear and she had no intention of discussing it.

Putting her life in Australia behind her had been easy in a big city with her high-profile career to keep her busy. And that's what she needed now. She didn't need dinner and question time with a country doctor.

'Here's the menu,' the young waitress said, as she placed the glossy card on the table for Laine. 'And we have some specials as well on the board over there. Can I get you a drink?'

Laine ordered a tonic and lime and glanced over the menu quickly, choosing grilled salmon. The waitress jotted down the order on her small pad, scooped up the menu and headed to the bar.

With a heartfelt sigh, Laine looked around the room. It was less noisy than the top pub but the locals were still engaged in friendly repartee and she could hear laughter and the clicking of billiard balls on the pool table in the next room. A dark purple-coloured out-back mural decorated part of one wall. The old chairs she remembered had all been replaced with new light-coloured wooden ones but the atmosphere hadn't changed. Taking a sip of her drink, which had arrived quickly, she hoped the food would be served quickly too.

Laine wanted to finish the shoot, leave Uralla and head back to New York. This was her last stop of the calendar assignment. Editing would take another two weeks, followed by a few weeks off, and then in March she would be heading to Rome. After that who knew where she would be? It didn't matter as long as she was on the go and not putting down roots anywhere. There would be another shoot for the American arm of FCTP towards the middle of the year and then back to Syd-ney for a quick visit for the annual fundraiser around Christmas. Sydney, she told herself, *not* Uralla.

Laine would always donate her time and money to the cause and enlist celebrity associates to raise the charity's profile as needed, but coming to this country town would never happen again.

Looking back now, Laine realised that returning here had been a huge mistake. Little about the town or even where she was sitting had changed. But she had. The monthly Sunday dinners that she had enjoyed with her adoptive parents in this same room had been such a treat. They had not been a wealthy couple but they'd had an abundance of love and they'd given it unconditionally to the girl who had come into their lives and they had become a family. Over time, the townspeople had *all* unofficially adopted the twelve-year-old girl of no fixed address as their own and she had grown to love each and every one of them.

The sound of her plate of grilled salmon and cutlery being placed on the wooden table pulled Laine back to reality. She smiled politely at the young waitress then dropped her eyes down to the food in front of her. The generous serving reminded her of where she was again. In New York, an enormous plate would hold a tiny salad with a sliver of salmon, no oil, no dressing, but here the generous salad, French fries and grilled salmon with home-made dressing threatened to spill over the equally ample plate.

Their food was as generous as their love, she mused before she chided herself for being ridiculous. It had to stop. Large plates with birdlike servings enabled her to fit into her jeans, she abruptly reminded herself. This size serving was not for her.

She knew she needed to finish and leave. As she quickly ate, she replaced outdated memories with thoughts of the next day's shoot. The McKenzies' property would be the perfect backdrop and with any luck she would have the second shoot with Pierce done in an hour or so. The sunrise over the paddock with the single eucalyptus tree would be perfect.

She was almost finished with both her planning and dinner when a tall shadow standing over her made her raise her eyes from her plate to see Pierce standing before her.

'Why lie? If you didn't want to have dinner with me, just say so. I didn't see a gun or a club in my hand when I asked.'

Laine saw the disappointment in his deep blue eyes. It wasn't anger, it was confusion but it was a cold glare nonetheless. She hurriedly swallowed the salmon she was chewing, wanting to somehow disappear into the carpeted floor. She felt terrible, suddenly riddled with remorse that she had both been caught and that she had upset this man she barely knew. He seemed like a genuinely nice man. And she couldn't remember the last time she'd felt anything that resembled guilt. That was because she didn't have room for remorse and, she hastily admitted to herself, because she had no one in her life who would bring about those feelings.

She just as quickly realised that she didn't like the feelings that were at threat of being awoken. The sleeping giant, her heart, she wanted left alone. Untouched in the watertight vault she had built. Laine Phillips had no room for anyone but herself. There was no room in her life for more than the occasional fling.

One night now and then with a handsome, no-strings-attached man to remind her that she was a woman. To allow her to feel the warmth of another body but never the warmth of another heart. Her New York sensibilities kicked in. She didn't want this man to stir up feelings that made her question her choices.

'Why did you bother following me? I decided that I'd rather eat alone and was being polite. The whole idea of twenty questions over dinner isn't my style. I'm a private person, always have been, and I don't see it changing any time soon.'

'Fine, eat alone. I was just trying to be polite and

show some country hospitality. And just for the record, I didn't follow you. My friends saw me walking back to my car after you ran out on me,' he said, not shifting his eyes from her but pointing to a group of men by the bar. 'I'd blown off our regular Friday night drinks with a lame excuse so I could have dinner with you. Guess it serves me right. Fastest karma ever.'

Without waiting for her response, Pierce left her sitting at her table and crossed to the bar to be greeted by the group. He kept his back to her. His broad shoulders seemed rigid and his stand was defensive, with his legs slightly apart and his arms folded. A couple of the men looked over at Laine and smiled. One raised his glass in her direction. She nodded back awkwardly.

Then suddenly she recognised one of them. It was Jim's eldest son, Mike. He hadn't changed much but, then, he'd already been a man in his twenties when Laine had left town. His resemblance to his father was strong, with thick brown wavy hair, deep blue eyes and an athletic build.

He did what Laine thought was a double take, and she watched him lean in and speak privately to Pierce. Her stomach dropped. Panic set in and her pulse began to race. Without hesitation she stood up, dropped her napkin on the plate and swiftly left the dining room, paying for dinner on her way out.

Her emotions were in turmoil.

Laine wasn't waiting around to find out if Mike had, in fact, realised she was an old family friend or if he was just talking about something unrelated with Pierce.

She was in a spin as she walked briskly down the street.

It was overwhelming. Being in this town and see-

ing old familiar faces was throwing her head first into
a melting pot of comfort, joy and pain. Wounds she'd
thought had healed, or perhaps buried, were suddenly
feeling very raw. Laine had pushed any emotion away
for so many years she had almost forgotten what it felt
like. Being numb had become a way of life for her.

But coming back now, she could almost physically
touch the kindness in the town. It was like an old blanket that could protect her if she allowed it to envelop
her. Unfortunately for Laine, accepting their kindness
would prise open her heart. And that could never happen. The way she lived her life now, there was no risk
of ever feeling pain. There was also a lack of joy in the
pure sense, but she found it to be a fair trade. No joy
but no also heartache.

She definitely preferred it that way. Life was easier.
And never suffering the incredible feeling of emptiness she'd endured at sixteen would be guaranteed if
she never opened her heart.

Laine unlocked the door to her motel room, stepped
inside and then slammed it shut on the world. The world
she'd once lived in and the one to which she knew she
could never return. She had to finish this assignment
and get the hell out of town.

Pacing her room as the bath filled, she questioned
her reasons for being there. *Was it a cruel act of the
universe that brought her to this town?*

CHAPTER THREE

THE ALARM RANG on her phone, waking Laine from a
deep sleep. It was a sleep that hadn't come easily so it
felt disappointing to be woken up. She sighed, rubbed
her eyes and rolled over in her tangled bedcovers to
check the time. It was four in the morning.

Climbing from her warm bed, Laine made her way
to the light switch and turned it on. She blinked as the
stark light hit her still blurry eyes. She had bathed the
night before so she just slipped into a pair of jeans, a
T-shirt and grabbed a leather jacket. It was summer
but the mornings still had bite. She chose some warm
socks and knee-high boots instead of her espadrilles as
she would be walking through the paddocks and that
could be messy. She threw on a scarf for good measure.

Knowing the motel restaurant wouldn't be open this
early, Laine had stopped at the supermarket on the way
home from dinner the previous night. Quickly she finished a banana, half a protein bar and a glass of orange
juice before she began the chore of loading the photographic equipment.

Pierce was fuming as he drove down the New England
Highway, heading towards the McKenzies' property.

He hadn't slept well at all. Livid described his mood. Getting out of bed at this godawful time for a woman as cold and dismissive as Laine Phillips brought his blood to the boil. But he knew that the shoot and in turn the fundraiser would be compromised if he didn't show up, so he had dragged himself out of bed, showered, shaved and dressed. Grudgingly, he also had to face the fact that it was Laine's face he'd pictured during his sleepless night.

Exactly who did she think she was? His jaw clenched as he remembered the feeling he'd had when he'd bumped into her into her having dinner alone. Walking out on him to eat dinner all by herself. It had been plain rude. He hadn't railroaded her into having dinner with him…or had he? He realised that arriving unannounced at her door hadn't given her much option other than to accept. But she seemed happy enough with the idea, he told himself, as he drove past her motel. He didn't want to look down the driveway but he did. And there she was. With the light spilling from her room and the glow from the full moon, he could make out all five feet four of her, alone and almost in the dark, lugging her equipment into the back of the rental car,.

He cursed as he swung the car back and drove towards her. *Little Miss Independence.* 'Here goes nothing,' he berated himself aloud. 'Prepare to be shot down again for trying to help!'

Suddenly the high beam of headlights heading down the driveway towards Laine's room blinded her. She put her hand up to block the glare.

'Need some help?'

Laine wasn't startled; she recognised the voice. She

had known it for only one day but it seemed very familiar. She hated that.

'I'm fine, really.'

Pierce jumped down from his four-wheel drive and reached for the heavy bag she was attempting to lift into the back of the car.

'I know you're perfectly fine on your own, you made that clear last night,' he retorted. 'But the sooner you're loaded and the shoot is over, the sooner I can get back to my patients. The first is at nine, so we need to get this circus on the road.'

Although, as his hand touched her soft skin, Pierce quickly realised he didn't want to get anything moving along. It felt warm against the cold of the morning. His mind wandered to how warm her entire body would be first thing in the morning lying next to him.

The thought of this irritating, argumentative, opinionated, gorgeous woman in bed with him was suddenly more appealing than any other thought he could muster. He had no idea what had come over him. His self-control was suddenly close to zero and he was always in control. There was something about Laine that puzzled and infuriated him. He didn't know what to make of her but she fascinated him like no other woman had ever before.

He gently tugged the bag free of her grip and placed it on the floor of the car beside the other equipment.

'Anything else?' he asked, looking around.

'No, that's it,' Laine replied, then matter-of-factly crossed the bitumen car park to close the door of her motel room. She was trying to ignore how good it had felt when his hand had touched hers momentarily. It had made her heart jump a little and her stomach turn in a curious, wonderful way. A way she had never felt before. She looked back in the moonlight at the man who was helping her and she suddenly wished her life was different.

He was so kind. Genuinely thoughtful and chivalrous. Not to mention more handsome than most models she had shot during her career. He was wearing black jeans, a white shirt untucked and a black leather jacket. Even without any effort on her behalf, she knew his shots would be stunning. The women would love him. He might not be the typical bad boy, but he had an edge.

The image was raw, the body was hot, but his eyes were warm and inviting. Summed up, the dream man. But the idea of accepting his kindness and giving it back was so at odds with how she lived her life. There was no room in her heart or her life for anyone. Besides, he wasn't her type. He was the staying kind. Nothing like the cold-hearted, indifferent bastards she dated. Those men made it easy to protect her heart. Leaving them before they left her was easy. She had done it enough times to know it was the best way for her.

Aware of other nearby guests still sleeping, Pierce closed the back of her car with a soft thud and headed back to his own.

'I'll follow you, then?' he asked, not wanting to have another argument. He was brutally aware that Laine was more independent than the fourth of July and needed, for some unknown reason, to call the shots, quite literally.

'Sounds like a plan,' she replied, before she climbed into her car, reversed into another parking space and turned the car round to face the street. Pierce followed suit and they were both on the New England Highway moments later.

Laine knew the area like the back of her hand. Although mindful of the interstate truck drivers who were hauling long loads through the night and into the early morning, she allowed her thoughts to return to the driver on her tail. She was confused as hell when it came to this man. With his looks, he could treat women badly and they would still flock to him, but he appeared to be gentleman.

She wished she could relax and enjoy his company but she couldn't risk it. She pushed the button to drop the electric window, needing air. Chewing nervously on her lips, she tried to return her focus to the road as she veered to the left and headed out to the property. In her rear-view mirror she saw the lights of Pierce's vehicle following her. Her focus waned as she pictured his strong, masculine hands firmly holding the steering-wheel and his hard, firm body pressed against the seat of his car. He was dangerously attractive. Thoughts of this country doctor that made her heart skip a beat had to end. He was off limits for so many reasons.

He'd surely had the perfect life, growing up, with two parents, a small dog, a white picket fence and siblings who were probably equally successful now they were grown up. A picture-perfect family photograph would have been sitting in a silver frame on the freshly dusted hallstand. Pierce would have arrived home from school to a mother in a floral apron, the smell of home-made raisin cookies baking in the oven.

Unlike her own childhood. More often than she cared to remember, Laine had arrived home from school to an empty house, a family she'd barely known, a tinned or frozen dinner she'd prepared herself and no time to do her homework because there had been so many chores with her name on them. And that had been her life in the better homes.

Then one wonderful day she'd found Maisey and Arthur Phillips. Two warm and uncomplicated people had opened their home and their hearts and had made her feel unconditional love for the first time in her life.

'Laine Phillips, you are so not his type,' she told herself. 'You don't bake apple pie and you don't do for ever—or anything even close to that. You rarely go on a second date.' Laine reminded herself this was a job, and she was doing it for the charity and those who would benefit. She gave her time as often as she could to help a cause so close to her heart. That had to be her focus for the next two days. Nothing more.

Fifteen minutes later, and after travelling along a long dirt road, they were at the property. Laine checked her watch. It was just after five. This would give her time to set up the shot and have Pierce positioned for the sunrise. She was mindful of the family still sleeping inside, so she dropped her speed and cruised past the house as quietly as possible and pulled up near a wire fence.

'I will need your shirt off again,' she called across the paddock as Pierce climbed from his car.

'Let's just do the open shirt instead,' Pierce called back as he unzipped his leather jacket. 'It's damned cold out here this morning.'

'No, I don't want a shirt, open or not,' she responded as she opened the back of the car and began pulling out her equipment. She left her headlights on and faced them away from the house and onto the area she would be setting up. 'The moment *I'm* ready to go, you need to remove both your jacket and shirt.'

Pierce couldn't believe the words that had come from her mouth. His blood was boiling. 'If you think you can order me about in the name of charity you've got another think coming. Not sure what your problem is, but you need to sort it out and get back to me because I'm sure as hell not hanging around here, listening to you.'

Laine watched him take off across the paddock to his car, praying he would not start the engine and leave.

'I'm sorry,' she called to him. 'Hate me, but please don't go. We need this shot for the calendar.'

He paused, and looked back at Laine. She was standing alone in the paddock with everything set up. Damn her. Angrily he pulled the keys from the ignition. A scowl washed over his face as he slipped the keys in his pocket and made his way back to the fence to the fence.

'Let's just get this over with,' he said as he slipped off his jacket and shirt.

Laine didn't answer him. She was so grateful that he had not driven off and she knew she would have deserved it if he had left. Somehow she seemed bent on offending him, and she knew it was not always conscious on her part. It was just something she did to keep people, particularly men, at arm's length.

In silence, she set up the camera tripod and the large gold reflector. That would capture the light and give Pierce's sculpted body a golden hue, almost sun-kissed, as the sun rose. She pulled the camera body from her bag and attached the lens, then directed Pierce to the wooden fence post before she returned to switch off the car headlights.

She was very aware that the sun would soon be peeking over the hill soon and there was an urgency to capture that one special shot. She held a small meter up close to Pierce to check the amount of light available and then returned to her position behind the camera.

'Almost perfect,' she called, as she pulled a tan stockman's hat and an atomiser from her large backpack and rushed over to him.

Without warning, she placed the hat on his black hair and sprayed his already cold body with a fine mist of oil.

'Are you mad?' he yelled as he pulled the hat free. 'I'm already bloody freezing and now you cover me in oil—what the hell is up with you?'

He stopped his rant the moment her warm fingers began working the oil all over his cold, muscled chest. He looked down to see both of her hands moving slowly but purposefully across his bare skin. His raised his gaze to look at her beautiful face.

Suddenly his emotions took over and he took her wrists with his hands. He said nothing, searching her eyes for a reaction before he pulled her up against his body and kissed her. She froze as he first pressed his lips down on hers then unwillingly she melted into his kiss. A moment before he had been so angry but now his lips met hers there was no anger, his kiss tender and passionate. For a brief moment she relished being that close to him. The desire he was stirring within her was undeniable and it felt so good. She didn't want it to end.

But she had to pull away.

'No...we can't.' She struggled to speak as she could still taste his mouth on hers. Her heart was racing as she pulled her emotions into line and her body away from his.

He released her immediately. 'It was just a kiss. I wasn't about to throw you onto the ground and ravage you in the crops...not yet at least.'

Laine didn't respond but her heart was still racing. Her stomach still churning. Her mind still spinning.

'We have to keep this professional—'

'You're absolutely sure about that?' his husky voice questioned her. 'Because that kiss didn't feel at all like work.'

Her breathing was still unsteady, just like her voice. 'You took me by surprise, but it can't happen again.'

'Why not? Is there someone waiting back in the Big Apple with your name tattooed on his chest?'

'No, it's not that.' Her eyes rolled at the thought.

'So there's no one I have to duel for you?'

Hardly, she thought. No man she had ever been with would fight for her. She doubted if any of them had given her a second thought after she'd ended their brief liaisons.

Laine closed her eyes for a moment before she answered. 'No one is waiting but that's not the point. This is work. I don't mix pleasure and work. Ever. It's a rule. So let's forget what just happened.'

Laine knew she would never forget the kiss. It would be impossible to erase the tenderness and passion in his lips. But she had to try.

Pierce decided to play it her way—for the moment at least. He would acknowledge her rule. Then do his best later to break it.

'Okay, have it your way.'

She smiled nervously before racing back to the camera. 'Don't touch your body and please put the hat back on,' she managed to tell him after she drew a deep breath to steady herself. *What was happening to her?* Very self-consciously she added, 'The mist looks like sweat. Believe me, you look great. Just hold still...'

Pierce ran his fingers through his hair and pushed the hat back on, still smiling from the kiss and his intention for it not to be the last one they shared. At just that moment the sun rose and the most beautiful colours spilled over the hills and across the paddock and Pierce was lit by the gold and tangerine rays. Laine had positioned Pierce so that the glare of the sun did not make him just a silhouette. The sun was on her right side and it bathed him in warmth. Still reeling from the kiss, she felt strangely different, and a little light-headed.

Unsure what to make of it, she dragged her thoughts as best as she could back to the job. Capturing the beauty of the sunrise. Nothing could compete with the magnificence of what Mother Nature brought to the table. No photo-editing program could ever capture the jaw-dropping beauty that she was witnessing. Her camera shutter was clicking at lightning speed, just like her heart, as she directed Pierce to use the old fencepost as a prop. The single eucalypt was a black silhouette in the background.

Laine was struggling with her emotions and the almost overwhelming desire to rush back and finish what Pierce had started, but she couldn't. She had to focus on framing the shot. It was perfect. She quickly checked that she was happy with the colour rendition and saturation, and ensured the shadows were not too dark.

December would without doubt be her favourite month in the calendar. Uralla was truly beautiful. And Pierce was more handsome than almost any man she had ever seen. And his kiss was more tender than any kiss she had ever received. But it would be the only one they would share. She could never let it happen again.

Laine was painfully aware that if she wasn't very careful she might run the risk of getting a little too close to the man leaning on the fencepost. And logic reassured her that it would only lead to disaster.

Pierce was physically cold, and clenching his teeth slightly to prevent them from chattering, but remembering the brief moment when his lips had met the warmth of Laine's made it bearable. Despite her pulling away, he had felt the way she'd instinctively responded. The way her body had pressed into his and the way she'd returned the kiss. Despite her icy demeanour, Laine had shown, albeit briefly, that she was all woman.

Pierce followed her directions. The focus and passion he witnessed as she released the camera from the tripod and moved freely on the ground near him, crouching and climbing as needed, kept the smile on his face. She was a complicated woman without doubt, but the love she had for her work was undeniable. It was as if she had opened a door and he was getting a view of the real Laine Phillips. And unfortunately for Pierce, he liked what he saw. And what he had felt in her kiss.

'That, as they say, is a wrap.' Laine tried to joke and remove the tension as she crossed to the car with her backpack. Once she put down the camera, she felt her shield had been removed. Hiding behind her professional demeanour was so easy with her camera in her hands.

She bit the inside of her cheek nervously as she stopped looking at Pierce through a lens and saw him standing so close to her. It was only a short time before that her body had been pressed against that nakedness. Pulling her desire into line, and her thoughts back to where they should be, she returned with a towel for Pierce. 'Here, take this and dry yourself off before you get dressed.'

Pierce had almost forgotten the cold. Watching Laine light up as she'd slipped into the role of professional photographer with ease, Pierce had felt an unexpected admiration. The way in which she had planned and executed the shoot had not only been skilled but also heartfelt in her desire to capture the beauty of the landscape.

And now he had felt her body against his, despite what she'd said about keeping things purely professional, she had definitely got under his skin. She was irritating, opinionated, abrupt and more defensive than any woman he had ever met, but it didn't deter him. In fact, he found that it spurred him on to know more about her. But time was limited. He was conscious that in just over twenty-four hours she would be gone. It gave him little time to be subtle.

He took the towel from her outstretched hand. 'Do you have any plans for dinner tonight?' he asked, then added for extra reassurance, 'No questions, just dinner.'

Laine stopped to consider the invitation. She wanted to say no, she knew in her head that she should say no, but something stronger, something she hadn't felt in years made her say yes. It was her heart talking again. This was the second time in as many days. What was it about Pierce that had her heart suddenly talking louder than her head? More than anything, she hated that she was listening.

She bit her lip and muttered, 'Okay. But on one condition...'

'Which is?'

'No repeat of what just happened. It can't happen again. This is just a calendar shoot, an assignment for me, that's all. There won't be another kiss.'

Pierce nodded. 'If that's the rule, I'll accept it.'

'Yes, it is.'

Pierce would accept it and then do whatever it took to *break* it. He wanted this beautiful, very talented conundrum more than he had ever wanted any woman.

'Okay.' He reiterated her low-key response as he slipped on his shirt and slowly buttoned it up, then put on his leather jacket. 'If we're finished up here, I'll head back to my surgery and see you out at the homestead around five.'

Laine was dismantling the reflector. 'Sounds good to me,' she said, alarm bells again ringing in her head. She was already questioning her sense in accepting the dinner invitation. 'Can you bring another pair of jeans? I'd like to shoot you in a faded old denim pair if you have one. Don't mind if they have rips in them—in fact, I'd prefer it if they did. The barn has a rustic feel and I'd like you to fit in with that.'

'Sure,' Pierce replied, and without thinking too much about it he began to help Laine put the equipment back in the car. They worked quickly and in moments both were ready to hit the road. It was still early and there were still no lights on in the house, which made Laine feel more relaxed. She would send an official thank-you note from New York and they would be none the wiser she had been there.

Pierce held back in his car so that Laine would exit the property first. There were still a few hours till he was needed at the surgery so he waved goodbye when they hit the New England Highway and headed home, planning on getting another hour's sleep.

Laine drove back to the Bushranger Inn, thinking about Pierce. The photos were great, she was sure. And he had been easy to shoot. She touched her mouth with her fingertips and thought back to the kiss and the way she had reacted. Her heart wished things could be different but they weren't. The idea of taking things further made her body sizzle with anticipation but her heart was now listening to reason. She couldn't afford to get involved. It wasn't in her plans. Not in Uralla, not anywhere.

She had another shoot that night and one she planned for early the next morning. Then she would be off. She'd be heading back to her real life in New York. The next day's shoot was for one of the major sponsors of the project and didn't involve Pierce. So after the session at the homestead and dinner there would be no further contact with him.

She drew in a deep breath and headed back down the highway. The sun was up now and there was a little traffic on the road but still not much. The driver of a small delivery truck waved at her as she passed him and she smiled and waved back. Her thoughts travelled back to her home and she smiled at the thought of the cab drivers leaning on their horns, a throng of people making their way down Wall Street, wrapped up against the freezing cold with a steaming coffee in one hand and their mobile phone in the other. Masses of people all heading to work, many in the same high-rise buildings with no time to stop and acknowledge each other. Their lives were frantic, stressful and for many, despite their social media updates, lonely.

Laine sighed as she remembered what she had left behind and what she had accepted in the trade. Manhattan was now home but Uralla was definitely tugging at her heartstrings. And a certain country doctor who certainly knew how to kiss was threatening to unravel her rules.

CHAPTER FOUR

'TREVOR JACOBS?' PIERCE called into the small waiting room. 'Please come in.'

The elderly man stood up slowly, folded his newspaper and slipped it under his arm before he crossed the room.

'G'day, Doc,' he said, as he entered the consulting room and took a seat.

'So, Trevor, what brings you to see me today?' Pierce enquired as he sat down and brought his patient's notes up on the computer screen on his desk.

Trevor drew a deep breath. 'It's the ticker, it's playin' up again. I was short of breath last night and again this mornin' and Betty reckoned I should get you to check it out.'

'Well, I'm glad you listened to your wife and came to see me,' Pierce remarked.

'As if I'd argue with Betty and live to see tomorrow.'

Pierce smiled. 'Okay, let's take your blood pressure and then I'll listen to your heart,' he said, reaching for the blood-pressure cuff. Wrapping it around the man's arm, he inflated it slowly and noted the result. 'And now if you could just unbutton your shirt?' Pierce began his examination. 'I need you to take a deep breath and hold it for a minute then slowly let it out. I just want to hear if there are any unusual sounds in your chest and also whether there's any build-up of fluid in your lungs.' After listening to his heart, he then lifted Trevor's shirt and placed the stethoscope on different places on his back, asking the older man to follow the same instructions. Then he checked the man's abdomen for swelling before he placed the stethoscope back on his desk and turned back to Trevor. 'One more thing then we'll be done. Can you just slip off your shoes and socks for a minute? I just want to check for any swelling.'

After completing the physical examination, Pierce washed his hands at the basin and returned to his desk.

'Is it bad?' Trevor asked, as he tucked himself in. 'Don't hold back, Doc, I can take it.'

Pierce considered the notes and turned his chair back to the man. 'It's nothing that we haven't discussed in the past, Trevor, but I want you to see a cardiologist in Armidale,' he began. 'Your heart appears to be struggling. It can't fill with enough blood or pump with enough force. The pumping action of your heart is getting weaker and that's why you are breathless and probably getting more tired.'

The old man nodded sheepishly. 'I'm exhausted by the day's end, sometimes exhausted by lunchtime. I've taken an afternoon nap a few times in the past couple of weeks.'

'I'm not surprised. Your heart is struggling to pump enough blood to the lungs, where it picks up oxygen, so that's why you're suffering from lethargy.'

'Lethargy? Isn't that some bug from air-conditioning units?'

Pierce looked at the man with a puzzled expression

for a moment then realised what he meant. 'Not legion-naire's, Trevor, lethargy. It means tiredness.'

'Good.' He laughed. 'Bloody hate to add another problem to me ticker not workin'!'

Pierce smiled but continued, his tone stern, 'Because your heart is weakened, blood and fluid can back up into the lungs, and some fluid can build up in the feet, ankles, and legs. Yours are showing signs of swelling.'

'But I've done everything you told me, honestly. Betty is one tyrant and won't let me have my bacon and eggs any more, won't let me put bloody salt on anything. We walk every day for about thirty minutes and I haven't had a smoke for near on twelve months.'

'I know you're doing everything I have asked of you but unfortunately you still have some problems. Your blood pressure is very high and you need to see the specialist as soon as possible.'

Trevor shook his head. 'So that godawful oat bran that she makes me eat for breakfast hasn't made a scrap of difference, then?'

'No, Trevor, I wouldn't say that. It's all helped but I would like you to go to the Armidale in the next few days for some tests.' Pierce began inserting the dif-ferent request forms into his printer. 'I'm ordering an ECG, which is a test to measure the rate and regularity of your heartbeat. The test can also show if the walls of your heart have thickened. I also want a chest X-ray to let me know whether your heart is enlarged or your lungs have fluid in them, both signs of heart disease, and I will ask for a blood test to measure the level of a hormone that increases in heart failure.'

'I'll feel like a lab rat at the end of that day, hey, Doc?'

Pierce signed each form as it was printed, knowing full well Trevor's humour was masking his concern.

'Trevor, they're routine tests and you've done everything I asked of you so let's get this done and refer you to a cardiologist at the New England District Hospital. Don't worry and let Betty know if she has any questions to call me.' With that he handed Trevor the printed forms and gently patted his back. 'I'll ask Tracy to call and make a time at the hospital for you as soon as possible and just keep doing what you are doing.'

The old man nodded and tried to smile but it was half-hearted and tainted by his anxiety as they made their way back to Reception.

'Betty's okay, I hope? It's unusual for her not to be here with you.'

'No, she's home with the grandkids today. To be honest, Doc, it was a relief to get out of there. I'm not sure how from three married sons we got five granddaughters, not a grandson in sight. Each one has a squeal louder than the other and they get vicious, really vicious over a bunch of scrawny-lookin' dolls. I don't know what to do with them. Trucks and cars, that's what I know, not prissy dolls.'

Pierce smiled and watched the older man shake his head as if he had spent the morning on a battlefield. He hoped one day to have a family of his own. Apart from his aunt, who kept in contact on the telephone, he had no living relatives.

Although the last two years in this town had made him almost forget that. He had made a great group of friends and had been a part of their lives, their family events, the odd Friday night watching televised sport, and Saturday afternoon watching the local football matches, summer barbeques, even birthday parties for their children. It was a close-knit community and just what he had been searching for. Pierce was very happy to call it home.

It was also a far cry from the life he'd known as child. A life far removed from what he wanted for his own children in the future. An Australian citizen by birth, he had travelled extensively with his parents and lived abroad for part of his childhood; seeing Paris by the age of four, Tokyo's largest theme park for his sixth birthday, New York every year until he was ten, and finally an exclusive boarding school in Germany shortly after the accident when everything had changed. Although he'd never wanted for anything material, and his parents had always been there for him while he'd been young, he'd missed having roots and stability.

Pierce took a deep breath, pushing back those memories, and instead thought about Laine. She seemed to love travel, waking up in different cities, surrounded by strangers on her photo shoots all over the world, while he wouldn't mind if he never used his passport again. They were two very different people, with very different lifestyles.

Their personalities were also at odds, but still the woman was entrenched in his thoughts. She was nothing like anyone he had met, and neither was her kiss. He wondered if she might be like a chocolate éclair— sweet and mushy if any man ever had the chance to break through the hard exterior. Unfortunately there was little time for him to be the man to cut through that tough coating.

They had the final shoot at the homestead at five o'clock. Pierce planned on heading into Armidale for a nice meal. Laine had been unnerved enough by something to run away from him at the top pub and the bottom pub hadn't fared much better so he thought a fresh start in the nearby town would be great. He didn't want a repetition of the previous disastrous evening. Armidale was only fifteen minutes away and the short trip would give him a little more time with this gorgeous Aussie export, if she would let him drive.

He spied his well-worn denim jeans in a bag by the door ready for the final shoot and the final time he would see Laine. It was a strange and inexplicable emptiness that crept up on him as he thought that in a few short days she would be back on the other side of the world and there was little chance their paths would ever cross again. But the warmth in her kiss made him want more at least while she was in the same town.

Laine spent the day in her room, sitting on the bed poring over that morning's shots. She had grabbed a late breakfast at the motel restaurant after she'd returned from the McKenzies' property, then at about twelve she headed out for some lunch and returned to the quiet confines of her room again.

She lay back on the bed and closed her eyes and thought about Pierce. She had been scrutinising his shots for hours and in each one he was more handsome than in the one before. There would be little editing needed, just as she had suspected during the shoots. The difficult part would be selecting only one photograph. His striking face, complete with chiselled jaw, sculpted abs and powerful arms, would melt any woman's heart, and he was definitely the perfect Dr December. Although they would only be able to imagine the passion in his kiss. She had experienced it first hand but it would be her secret for ever. The tenderness and passion when he'd stolen that kiss would not be easily if ever forgotten.

He would indeed be a wonderful Christmas present for every woman who bought the calendar.

She wondered why there wasn't a Mrs Beaumont. Perhaps he was a confirmed bachelor, she mused, or just didn't want to settle down until he was older. She had seen the details on the registration form and had noted he was thirty-four. Still young enough to leave marriage for a few years, she thought.

'And why exactly that is your concern?' she muttered under her breath as she sat up, crossed her legs and twisted her hair into a high bun, securing it with a pencil. She hoped that changing her posture would bring the blood back to her brain, away from her heart, and stop her stupid train of thought. 'It was only a kiss and it will do no good thinking about a man like Pierce,' she berated herself. 'Love is for fools.'

'This is Dr Pierce Beaumont. I would like to speak with the paediatric resident regarding an infant admitted earlier today ago with suspected pertussis, James Hollis.' Pierce waited to be connected to the paediatric ward.

'This is Myles Oliver, the attending paediatrician looking after James.'

'Hi, Myles, Pierce Beaumont, the Hollis family GP in Uralla. Just wanted to see how James doing.'

'Thanks for getting James to us so quickly, Pierce. He's stable, we've him isolated from other patients and I've just broken the news to his mother that he may be with us for a few weeks. The coughing has become progressively worse over the last two hours so we have rostered nurses to watch him constantly for the next twenty-four hours. We're monitoring his heart and breathing.'

'So pertussis is the diagnosis?'

'Yes, there's a spate of whooping cough around at the moment. There's quite a few cases in the New England Tablelands region. It happens when some people in the community refuse vaccinations and, bingo, the society's immunity declines. Typically, it's the little ones like James who suffer.'

'What's your treatment plan?'

'Monitoring and antibiotics. He's still breastfeeding but if that slows he'll be given IV fluids. I'm keeping a close watch on the oxygen therapy.'

'Please keep me posted. I will try to get there tomorrow and see how his mother is dealing with it all. She'll need some support.'

'Great. See you then.'

Pierce hung up the phone and walked out to the waiting room.

'Tracy, can you block off a bit more time around lunch tomorrow? I want to check on James Hollis and his mother in Armidale.'

Tracy checked the diary for the following day. 'Not a problem, I can shift a couple of appointments around.'

CHAPTER FIVE

LAINE HEADED OUT past the Armidale airport to the homestead a little earlier than she needed to be. She loved the grounds and the ambience of Saumarez and she knew it would be months, if not years, before she was in a place so serene again.

As she drove along the narrow dirt road leading to the homestead gate, she gazed out at the wide-open paddocks dotted with small groups of cows taking shelter from the afternoon sun under the towering eucalypts. There were about fifteen other farm buildings on the ten-hectare grazing property and for obvious reasons it was a popular wedding venue. Laine could see why couples would choose the stunning backdrop.

However, she couldn't understand why they would want to get married. Signing up to depend on one person for the rest of your life was sheer madness, she had decided long ago. There was only one person in the world who would never let Laine Phillips down or make her feel secure then cut the rope, and that was herself. Laine Phillips was her own life partner and twelve years ago she made the only vow she'd told herself she would ever make, and that was to never depend on anyone else.

Still, it was a wonderful day and she wanted to enjoy the serenity of the town while she could. She shook herself back into appreciating her wonderful surroundings. In no time at all she would be on another plane, beginning the long haul home to her high-rise apartment, so she decided to make the most of the open spaces.

It was very peaceful. She lowered the electric window and breathed in the warm, clean air. It took her back to a time when this had been all she'd known. No hustle and bustle, no traffic fumes, no rush to be anywhere and definitely no planes to catch.

Laine thought back to her very first plane trip at eighteen years of age. It had been an assignment she had secured for a small indie music magazine, photographing a grunge band in Melbourne. She hadn't wanted to admit to her boss that she had never flown before. Her nerves had mounted as she'd sat in the departure lounge, her boarding pass clutched in her shaking hand, but she'd known that if she wanted to forge a career overseas then she had to take the flight.

Her knuckles had been white and her stomach halfway up her throat when the plane had finally built up speed as it had thundered down the runway. When the huge and, in her opinion, much too heavy plane had finally become airborne, Laine's heart had pounded in her chest with such ferocity she'd thought it might possibly burst. She'd felt so light-headed that she'd doubted there had been any blood left in her brain. The fact that she hadn't passed out had been a miracle. But she hadn't, and it had been the first of literally hundreds of trips she was to make in the coming years. First they'd got longer and then they'd become a better class and over the years Laine had became accustomed to the business lounge in the international airports. But whenever the tyres of the plane lifted off the ground, she became Melanie Phillips for a few short minutes and wished there was another hand holding hers.

She came to a halt at the end of the gravel and dirt driveway as she found a place to park down near the closest of the large barns. It was Thursday and there were tourists, and probably some locals, she assumed, taking a guided a tour of the Edwardian mansion's thirty rooms and enjoying a leisurely stroll through the picturesque cottage garden, the picking garden and over the perfectly manicured lawns. But it was the out-buildings, complete with antique tools and equipment, that held more interest for Laine. They were a link to early pastoral life and would be a perfect backdrop for her final rustic shoot with Pierce.

She notified the caretaker of her arrival and then headed off to unpack her equipment and begin loading it inside the barn. The large door on the opposite side was open and the sweeping view was as breathtaking as Laine remembered. After stacking her equipment in one of the small rooms inside the barn and locking her car, she stood in the doorway and looked out across the paddocks. The other smaller outbuildings held farm equipment and the one closest was a chicken run filled with large Rhode Island reds.

Laine had been fourteen when she'd last stood in the very same place. It had been a wedding, a real barn wedding complete with white tables and chairs, home-made jam with checked gingham tops as wedding favours and a lot of dancing. She remembered her mother and father laughing as they'd danced all evening. With the back of her hand she wiped away a tiny tear that had formed at the corner of her eye. This was becoming a habit that she didn't much like.

'A penny for your thoughts?'

Laine knew the voice only too well. Dr December had also arrived early at Saumarez. She had no intention of letting him see her upset.

'I was at a wedding here many years ago. The bride was a local girl and the groom was a musician from Tamworth. It was one of the best times I had as a child,' she said honestly, and without turning around, before she dropped her voice to not much more than a whisper. 'Although, to be honest, it was so long ago I can only just remember the details.'

Pierce didn't hear the soft words she had muttered as he studied the silhouette in the doorway. She was still in her jeans and shirt but in the warm afternoon sun there was no sign of the morning's jacket or scarf. Her long wavy hair was hanging down over her shoulders and her feet were in flat brown sandals. Even without seeing her pretty face, Laine was still demanding his attention.

Her emotions back under control, she suddenly spun on her flat heels. 'So what brings you here so early?'

'I could ask you the very same question,' he returned, as he looked into the most stunning green eyes he had ever seen. Each time he looked at her face he found her more beautiful than before.

'Setting up for the shoot.'

Pierce looked around the empty, dusty barn complete with cobwebs strewn across the beams and smiled. 'Yep, this place is certainly filled with your equipment. Can't find a place to stand without tripping over a cord or light.'

Laine knew he had seen through her and decided to turn it into a factual conversation fuelled by her high-school studies as she turned around dismissively to the panoramic view again. 'Did you know that the property takes its name from the Dumaresq Estate in Jersey in the Channel Islands and it was the last stopping point for settlers moving north?'

'Yes, I did,' he replied in an equally controlled voice. 'And did you know that after Dumaresq's death the property was sold to a gentleman by the name of Thomas, whose family lived in the original slab homestead overlooking Saumarez Creek?'

'Fine,' she retorted, 'Mr Know-It-All, when was it built?' Laine didn't actually know the date or the last piece of information that Pierce had provided so this question was for her own interest and she couldn't verify his answer if her life depended on it.

'The date is somewhere around the early nineteen hundreds. There is nothing recorded to confirm the exact date.'

Intelligent and good looking, she thought to herself. A lethally tempting combination.

'I'm assuming we can't shoot with all of the visitors still around, so what if we have something to eat at the homestead café? They have the best scones, jam and cream.'

Laine was tempted. She knew the cream would be country rich, the jam would be home-made and the scones would be freshly baked. She had a mental picture of the steam escaping from the fluffy dough as she cut it open and covered it with fresh, fruit-laden jam and a huge dollop of freshly whipped cream. Her mouth was watering with the images in her head but she also knew that it went against everything her personal trainer would allow—no carbs, only low-fat dairy and no refined sugar. She bit her lip and knew there was only one choice to make.

'Do you think they'd have blackberry jam?'

Pierce nodded. 'Only one way to find out.'

The time passed quickly in the homestead café. Pierce didn't ask any questions relating to Laine's past and instead kept the conversation to her work and his role as one of the town's doctors.

'So what's the population here now?' she enquired, finishing the last bite of her delicious afternoon tea.

'Around twenty seven hundred, give or take.'

Laine was surprised. The town had had nowhere near that number when she'd left. It had grown but she knew it hadn't changed. Only she had and that was her issue.

'I think I'd better set up my equipment and you should put on something a little scruffy for this shoot.'

He playfully saluted her. 'The ripped jeans are in my car.'

In a different universe, she thought, this could end very differently. The handsome, eligible, intelligent, charismatic man sitting opposite her might ask her out, she would without hesitation say yes, and they would at the very least kiss goodnight in a few hours' time. But here and now they were two different people and it would end with a handshake after dinner tonight. No ifs, no buts. He was a charming man, with a good heart, and yet it would never work. It could never happen. They were so very different, although she noticed during their conversation he was as guarded about his past as she was about hers.

Not that she pried, but it was as if he hadn't had a life before he'd arrived in Uralla. Well, at least not one he cared to share with her. It seemed odd for a country doctor to be equally unwilling to talk about his past. There couldn't be anything too shocking or dark, she mused, or he wouldn't be able to practise medicine. He didn't appear overly scarred or bitter, unlike her, but she decided but there was definitely something Pierce Beaumont was hiding.

'Perfect,' she said as she took another shot. 'Now just lift your chin a little and lean back into the doorway.

Pierce followed Laine's instructions and she was able to capture the setting sun and the handsome subject, doing justice to both.

'Final shot now the sun's almost gone. Can you reach out and touch each side of the doorway,' she asked, as she lay on the ground, shooting up at his glistening torso. 'It looks amazing from here.'

Pierce couldn't help but agree as he looked at Laine lying on the ground in front of him. Her hair was cascading across the cobbled floor like a luxurious pillow and her long legs were poured into her tight blue jeans. Her white shirt was a little dusty and slightly open, revealing her lightly tanned cleavage in her white lacy bra. It took every ounce of self-control not to drop to the ground, pull her into his arms and kiss her again. And then more. The level of desire this woman was stirring in him was driving him crazy. But he had agreed to her rules. And he had to keep his word, even though it was killing him.

'Great job,' she announced, getting to her feet and dusting herself off. She ran her fingers through her hair and shook it gently. 'I may have picked up a little something from the floor but, what the heck, it will brush out and I have some amazing shots.'

Pierce was steeling himself against the doorframe. He took a deep and calculated breath and tried to keep his longing for the woman, so dangerously close to him, in check. 'I thought we might hit an authentic Italian restaurant in Armidale. Great pasta, the best wine and gelato better than you would find in Napoli.'

Laine stretched her back from side to side and then tucked in her dusty shirt. 'Sounds lovely but I think the way I look that we should go for drive-through hamburgers.'

'It's still early, we have time to change...' he began.

'Time maybe but I'm exhausted and lacking any energy to find fresh clothes in my suitcase and then head out again. It's been a long few weeks since I arrived in Australia and I could really do with a hot bath and an early night.'

Pierce wasn't about to accept her answer that quickly. 'Then what about the Chinese restaurant? It's a far cry from the Waldorf, so they won't mind how you're dressed. I'll stay in my ripped jeans if it would make you feel better.'

Laine smiled at his dining comparison. It was much better than the idea of heading out after her relaxing bath to find food. A quick meal on the way home would be the easier option.

'Sure. Why not?'

'Great. I'll help pack this all up and head to the club.'

Laine was already packing away her gear and feeling more tired by the minute. 'I'm sure I'll crash tonight and sleep for ten hours!'

They worked in unison, wrapping cords, packing up lights and putting everything away neatly in the allocated waterproof bags. Laine was grateful for the assistance and she couldn't help but notice how carefully Pierce handled everything. He was respectful of her belongings. That made her smile, just a little, as she zipped up the final bag.

'I'll follow you,' Laine said, as she closed the car door on the last of the gear and looked back at the tree-lined horizon one last time. Even in the dimming light it was stunning in its raw simplicity and she hoped with all her heart that she had captured the natural beauty of the land.

Pierce climbed into his dusty four-wheel drive, and headed out of the car park, along the windy dirt road and onto the New England Highway. He glanced back more than once, much more than once, at the car following him, wishing that the driver would stay a little longer in his town.

Fifteen minutes later the two cars pulled into the car park.

Laine jumped out of the car, hungry and tired in equal amounts. The evening was getting cool so she pulled her favourite designer sweater from her backpack and threw it over her shoulders. A quick Chinese meal, a goodbye, thank-you-very-much handshake with Pierce and then bed for a good night's sleep was Laine's plan. She pushed the image of their kiss from her mind. That would never happen again. Pierce had been professional during the shoot and she was relieved he hadn't tried a repetition of the early morning embrace when his lips had met hers so passionately. She wasn't sure she could pull away a second time.

'Let me get your backpack—you don't want to leave your laptop in the car.'

Laine looked at the man who was being so gallant. Most of the men she spent time with socially wouldn't give a damn about her possessions. Or even her for that matter, not truly.

With one hand in the small of her back and the other holding her backpack, he gently directed her to the door. It felt so good for him to feel the warmth of her body through her thin shirt. He knew he couldn't let his fingers rest there too long but he didn't want to pull away until the last possible moment.

Laine rested back a little into the softness of his warm hand. It felt good. His touch was strong but gentle. She didn't want him to move his hand away but she couldn't let him know that.

They entered the back way and climbed a flight of stairs into the bistro. It was busy for a Thursday night and they sat at the end of a long table. A number of patrons waved at Pierce and he acknowledged them in a similarly friendly manner. Laine was happy to be sitting away from the main crowd. She still felt a little uncomfortable in case anyone recognised her but with only Friday's shoot for one of the major sponsors in Armidale ahead of her, she was feeling a little more relaxed.

'White wine or something a little stronger after the day you've had?' Pierce asked with a teasing wink.

'My day was fine and quite easy,' she replied lightheartedly. 'To be honest, I'd rather stick to chilled sparkling water with a twist of lime.'

Pierce crossed to the bar and ordered the drinks while Laine looked over the menu.

Moments later he placed in front of her a tall glass

with sparkling water, ice and a lime quarter sitting precariously on the rim. 'Spied anything you fancy?'

Laine thought better than to admit the truth. She
fancied Pierce Beaumont. Laine Phillips, who travelled
the world for a living, who refused to put down roots
for more than a few weeks, the same woman who had
a no-second-date rule, fancied the small-town doctor.
It was ludicrous. And it wasn't going to happen. She
had to finish dinner, shake hands and leave him at her
motel-room door. It couldn't go any further, although
the idea of spending the last night in town in Pierce's
warm, strong arms was very appealing.

But Laine knew it couldn't happen. The night would
no doubt be wonderful, he was such a caring man with
a body that rivalled Adonis', and she suspected from the
kiss that his skills as a lover would be perfectly honed,
but then there was facing waking up in the morning.
That awkward moment when she had to ask him to
leave and say she would never see him again. She had
done it more than once before and it had been easy, but
this time she suspected it might actually hurt a little.
It might be sad, it might even make her cry, and Laine
Phillips didn't want any pain or sadness in her life.

She had to keep it friendly. But that was it.

'Special fried rice and lemon chicken sounds great
to me.'

'I'm a black bean beef type of man so I guess that's
our order done. Sit tight and I'll be back.'

Laine watched him walk away and this time she noticed the slight swagger in his long, purposeful steps.
His broad shoulders, slim hips and perky rear could
not be overlooked. He was the most handsome man in

the bistro and from the way the women's eyes followed him she wasn't the only one who noticed.

The calendar would walk off shelves if he was the doctor for every month. Laine knew there would be no complaints if each of the twelve pages contained a different shot of her gorgeous dinner companion.

'So, no talk of the past,' he said as he sat down again. 'I learnt that early on, and I don't want you to walk out on me, so let's talk about the future. Where do you see yourself in five years' time?'

Laine sipped her icy cold drink and contemplated the question for a few minutes. 'I honestly don't know. I don't tend to think long term but I suspect doing much the same. Although I would like to increase my charity work. I believe in certain causes and in general they aren't high profile or on anyone's political radar and receiving oodles of money. So if I can help, I will.'

Pierce knew the woman sharing the table was a bundle of contradictions. She had an opinion about almost everything but she loved to listen; she tried to be cold and distant but she worked for charities that no one else cared about; she chose to be behind the camera when she was gorgeous enough to be on a magazine cover; and she had a deep appreciation of the Australian landscape and this little town in the middle of nowhere but chose to live in a high-rise apartment in one of the busiest cities in the world.

And he was confused, intrigued, curious but above all smitten. Laine Philips was fascinating for so many reasons and each minute he spent with her made him want her a little bit more.

But he couldn't let her know for fear of her bolting before her rice arrived.

CHAPTER SIX

LAINE RESTED HER head back and closed her eyes for a moment. She was in heaven.

'Was it as good for you as it was for me?' Pierce asked in a low, husky voice.

'Better, I suspect, much better.'

Pierce smiled. 'Maybe next time I'll have the chicken too, then. But mine was still great and the fried rice here is always good.'

She opened her eyes and looked at Pierce. 'Glad you talked me into coming here for dinner. With a belly this full I shall sleep like a little pig in mud now.'

Pierce chuckled. 'Bet you don't use that expression around your Manhattan friends, they'd have no idea what—'

His conversation was interrupted by a loud commotion by the doorway and then the sound of screeching tyres.

'Hell, no!' came a man's voice from the stairwell. 'I'll get the bastards who did this.'

Pierce stood up and, like most of the patrons in the bistro, made his way over to see what was happening.

'Sons of bitches. I'll rip their bloody arms off when I find them,' came another voice at top pitch.

'Any idea what's happening?' Laine called out in a concerned voice, hoping Pierce had seen something.

He shook his head in reply before he moved into the stairwell and out of her sight as he followed the men downstairs. As soon as he reached the ground he knew what had happened. It looked like a demolition yard. Almost every vehicle in the car park had been damaged. Windows were smashed, hoods and panels were dented and there were rubber burn marks on the bitumen leading away into the street. It appeared to have been more than one carload of perpetrators that had done the damage and sped away.

Pierce could see that the driver's door of his SUV had been scratched but it looked like they had been disturbed before they'd finished their handiwork on his. He looked over at Laine's hire car. The rear-view mirror was hanging down, with only wires keeping it attached, the front and back windscreen and the windows on the passenger side had been smashed. He raced over, fearing the worst. It was quickly confirmed.

All Laine's equipment was gone from the car. Everything had been taken, dragged out through the broken windows. He looked around on the ground and lying in the pile of shattered glass he saw two of her bags with the contents strewn across the bitumen. The lights had been trampled and the shards of broken glass were mixed with the glass from the windows. A tripod lay buckled and broken by the tyre and two camera lenses had been smashed against the building wall.

His head dropped into his hands. Laine would be devastated. He knew this equipment was very important to her. She had such pride and valued it all. To her, they were more than just work tools, she had an affinity and love of these objects.

The crowd outside was growing with all the bistro patrons pouring out to assess the damage. Something like this had never happened in the town, let alone this family-friendly restaurant car park.

'Did anyone see anything, anything at all?' an older woman, who Pierce recognised as one of the teachers at the local school, pleaded as she approached her car. It had been painted with a spray can of black paint. The roof had been smashed in, the tyres slashed and every window broken. It appeared to have taken the brunt of the attack. 'Who would do something so vicious? For no reason.'

'I saw them speed off, but they were too quick for me to get their number plates. I know they're not from around here, never seen them before,' one of the local lads told her.

'There were at least three carloads,' another older man added. 'That's why they were able to do so much damage so quickly. Rotten hooligans must have been driving through and decided to smash up some cars just because they could.'

Pierce quickly realised by the number of beer cans on the ground that it had been an alcohol-fuelled spree of destruction. 'Let's hope the driver wasn't drinking as much as it appears the rest were.'

'Oh, my God, what happened?' Laine gasped, as she reached the car park with the last of the bistro patrons. Then she spied her car. 'No, not my equipment, tell me it's not gone.' She looked at Pierce for reassurance he couldn't provide.

'I'm so sorry,' he said as he crossed to her. He wanted

to almost barricade her from the desecration of her belongings. Pierce instinctively wrapped his arms around her, pulling her close as she saw everything lying smashed on the ground.

'Why? What sort of people do this?' She paused. It suddenly felt so natural to be in the warmth of his embrace. For a fleeting moment she felt a level of comfort that she had not experienced in over a decade. The softness of his chest, the strength of his arms wrapped around her made her feel protected. She felt safe for the first time since she'd left the town all those years ago. Her belongings were gone but somehow he made it almost okay. But she had to snap out of it. Quickly she reminded herself that she didn't want this feeling of dependence. She was used to facing life's challenges alone. Pierce was not her saviour. She could save herself.

Abruptly, she broke free of his hold and marched around to inspect the damage. She grew angrier with every step. 'The bastards have taken my cameras and smashed everything else.'

Pierce was inspecting the damage when the screeching of tyres sounded not too far away and then the sound of buckling metal. He rushed to the road to see the car had spun and hit a metal power-line pole on the main highway. The impact had been so great the rear of the car was completely crushed. Three other men raced with him to the scene.

'It's one of the hoodlum's cars. They must have turned around and be heading back Tamworth way,' one of them said loudly.

Pierce looked both ways on the highway before he

crossed with two of the men. Laine looked on anxiously from across the road.

'Stop,' someone called to Pierce as he approached the car. 'The fuel line must have been severed on impact, there's petrol leaking onto the road.'

Pierce saw the fuel slowing pouring from underneath the car. It was trickling towards the front of the car and the heat of the engine. He also saw the driver slumped over the steering-wheel. Quickly he prised open the driver's door, only to stop as flames could be seen emerging from the other side of the car.

'Step back,' the man called again. 'She's about to go up.'

Pierce could see the flames but he could also see the driver. He looked not more than sixteen and he was unconscious. There was no way that Pierce would walk away. If he didn't get him out, the boy would certainly die.

'He'll never make it,' another man called out. 'Get back away from the car.'

Pierce continued to struggle with the door until finally it opened. With only seconds to spare he pulled the young man from the car. As the boy's feet hit the bitumen the interior of the car was filled with the flames that had been lurking under the chassis. The other men rushed over and lifted the driver's legs and assisted Pierce to carry him across the road to safety.

'You're bloody crazy,' the older man said. 'He was one of the hooligans.'

In silence Pierce stared back at the car now engulfed in flames. His brow became clammy and his breathing laboured for a moment. Laine rushed over to see Pierce run his hands through his hair and watch in silence as the fire slowly took over the entire car, reducing it to a ball of fire and smoke. For a split second he was preoccupied, almost as if he was somewhere else completely. His far-away look didn't go unnoticed by Laine.

Abruptly Pierce turned his attention away from the burning vehicle and back to the young man. He knelt down and checked his vital signs. 'Can someone call for an ambulance and the firies, if you haven't already? Here's hoping there were no spinal injuries because I didn't have time to brace him.'

'Forget spinal injuries, he's bloody lucky to be alive, thanks to you,' the older man said, shaking his head in disbelief at what he had just witnessed.

Pierce checked the young man's airway before beginning CPR. The smell of alcohol was so strong on the boy that Pierce wasn't surprised he had lost control of the car. Laine watched on in awe at the way Pierce was handling the situation. He had risked his life for a young man who had been one of the group that had vandalised the cars. They had damaged everything in sight without remorse and yet he hadn't judged the boy's actions, he had saved his life. Completely selflessly he had stayed when he'd been told to run. The young man from the wrong side of the tracks owed his life to Pierce.

Pierce continued CPR until the ambulance arrived and the paramedics took over.

Laine doubted that she had ever seen such generosity of spirit in her life. Pierce was not just a handsome country doctor. He was a hero.

CHAPTER SEVEN

'YOUR TYRE IS slashed. Let me drive you back to the motel at least and we can get the hire company out to collect the car tomorrow.'

Laine looked down at the flat tyre. The shattered glass that had surrounded the car had been swept away, she assumed by the owners of the restaurant and no doubt the locals had chipped in to help out. Her torn bags and broken equipment had been placed neatly on the back seat. The car park mess had, for the most part, been cleaned up. She had forgotten how a small community rallied round and helped out. A mess like this would sit in a New York street until municipal services came and cleaned it up. She knew the foot traffic would turn up their noses and walk on by.

'Thank you, that would be great,' she said. 'I guess I can sort it out in the morning. It's not like there's anything worth taking now. It's all broken.'

All the commotion had finally subsided. The local fire truck and police had arrived on the scene at the same time. The fire had been quickly extinguished just as the rescue helicopter had airlifted the young man to hospital with head and suspected internal injuries. The police had taken statements and hoped, with the assistance of the injured young man in the days to come, all the culprits would be located and charged.

Not quite the evening Laine had imagined. Standing in the quiet of the car park with Pierce, she suddenly remembered she had a sponsor shoot the next morning at the local branch of a large national bank. 'Damn, my camera and my lights, I need them for tomorrow and they're gone. Thank God all of your shots are on the USB in my bag but everything I need for the sponsor shoot is gone and I have no way to get replacements here by tomorrow.'

'What if you purchase new gear at the camera shop in Armidale?'

'I can look into it but they may not stock everything I need. A lot of it comes from the overseas supplier directly. I can have it shipped but it will take a couple of days and the bank will be closed until Monday—'

'Tuesday, actually,' Pierce interjected.

'Tuesday?'

'It's a public holiday on Monday. Australia Day, so everything's shut.'

Laine just shook her head. 'But I need to be back in New York by then.'

'Then you'll have to miss the photo shoot in Armidale. No biggie. I guess it's just a country bank.'

'Don't say that,' she retorted. 'I promised the sponsor and I don't break promises. Whether the bank is in Wall Street or in Armidale, I said I would shoot it. And I will. I'll just have to make some changes to flights and get whatever equipment the Armidale camera shop doesn't have shipped to me from Sydney. Then let the bank know it won't be happening tomorrow. It can be done.' Laine was more than experienced at thinking on her feet.

'Great, then let's get you back to your motel so you can start making your calls and sending your emails.' He was still functioning a little on adrenalin and knew it would subside slowly, as would the vivid images that had come rushing back when he'd watched the fire envelop the car.

On the drive back to her motel Laine searched the net on her phone in silence but all the while was thinking about the way Pierce had looked back at the burning car. She wasn't sure she had a right to ask but something was making her want to know more about the man who had by his actions unwittingly proved himself to be so very different from the man she had imagined him to be.

'What happened back there?' Laine suddenly asked, as Pierce pulled the car to a halt in the car park at the front of her room.

'Running sheet, well, the vehicles in the car park were wrecked by some very troubled teens and then one wrapped himself around a pole, the car caught on fire and the young man was airlifted to hospital. But no one died so all in all a good outcome. Did I miss anything?'

'That's not what I meant,' she said. Undoing her seatbelt and turning towards Pierce, she brought her legs up onto the seat. 'I meant with you. I saw the look on your face as you watched the flames. It definitely wasn't fear, you'd just pulled the boy to safety, but there was something. I could see it in your eyes when you looked back at the burning car. I'm right, aren't I?'

Pierce turned his head to face his still slightly dusty

driving companion. She was an amazingly beautiful woman but a woman with a question that begged for an answer. An answer he had never given before but one he now thought he might be ready to share. He hadn't struggled with the fire the way he'd imagined he might. The need to free the young man had been greater than the fear of the fire. Finally perhaps he had put that to rest.

He took a deep breath, put down the electric window and felt the evening breeze on his face. He said nothing as he gathered his thoughts.

'If you'd rather not talk about it, I understand. I really have no right to ask.'

'No, it's okay. I've never spoken about it and I guess I should and I suppose a car park is as good a place as any.' He lifted his gaze to the beauty of the now darkening sky. He didn't really notice the clouds that had formed streaks across the charcoal backdrop. His thoughts were travelling to a time in his past as he rubbed his neck.

'It goes way back. I was twelve, and I was with my parents in New York. It was November. My father liked to spend Thanksgiving there every year and watch the Macy's parade. We were staying in our condo, as we always did, and there was an explosion in the kitchen. They found out later it was a gas leak, my mother and father...' He paused for a moment. 'They were killed instantly. I had no idea at the time—'

'Oh, my God,' Laine gasped, and instinctively covered her mouth with both hands, her eyes wide in horror.

'The fire spread quickly,' Pierce continued matter-of-factly as his hands ran across the steering-wheel.

'I was forced out onto the balcony. We were fifteen stories up and the firies told me I had to jump. The ladders couldn't reach me and so I had no choice.'

'So you were alone on the balcony?'

'No, our neighbour's dog, Jackson, had been staying with us while they were away. He'd run through the smoke and found me, so I grabbed him as the fire took hold of the room behind us. When I saw the curtains finally go up in flames I climbed onto the railing and looked down at the fire trucks and the safety net below and I was petrified. I still remember fear running through me and the feeling of lead in my legs. They looked so small and so far away down on the pavement.

'I had no idea where my parents were and finally decided they must have left through the front door somehow. I'd been waiting for them to come and get me but the flames were too close and there was no sign of them. The idea that Jackson and I could die made me realise that I had to jump with him. No matter how frightened *I* was, I had no choice, I had to save him. So I stepped off the railing and just hoped to God they caught us both.'

Laine drew her legs closer to her chin and shook her head in disbelief. Pierce had been through so much and she had mistakenly thought his life had been easy. His words cut like a knife. How dared she have judged him on first sight? He hadn't judged the young man tonight. Instead, he had risked his life for a troubled young man he didn't even know. She had a lot to learn, she realised. And a lot she needed to forget.

Her illusions had been shattered and she was disappointed beyond belief with herself. The man she had imagined him to be had been one who had enjoyed a happy, secure family life, and it couldn't be further from the truth. She had envied him for something that he had never had. In fact, she had been more fortunate in having her parents until she'd turned sixteen, when they had been taken from her. She had been almost an adult and Pierce had only been a child when he'd lost his mother and father. And yet he never wore it on his sleeve. He didn't appear to be bitter with the world and yet he had every right to be an angry man.

'Hey, don't go quiet on me now,' he said, noticing her serious expression. 'It was a long time ago, over twenty years, in fact, and after tonight I guess I'm okay with fire, so I just need to work a bit on the height thing and I'll be as good as new.'

'And that's why you didn't want to go up the ladder. I'm so sorry,' she began, with concern etching her voice. 'If I'd known I would have found another way. I wish you'd told me. I thought you were just trying to be difficult. I must have come across as such an insensitive bitch.'

Laine wanted to reach out to him but not from pity—and neither was it the feeling that both owning the title of adult orphan made them in a way kindred spirits. It was more than that. It was his willingness to help another human being without hesitation. No preconceived ideas or prejudice despite what he had been though himself. And then to be willing to share something so personal with her. It took courage to be that vulnerable, that exposed, and she felt close to him for that reason alone. She had not witnessed that level of honesty in many years. Particularly not from herself. There was so much more to this country doctor than she had ever imagined.

'I didn't mean to go all serious on you.'

'Good. Now at least when you head back to the Big Apple you won't remember the Aussie doc as a pain in the arse without reason.'

'Far from it.' Laine's mouth curved into a smile and she leant over and did something she had never done. She tenderly kissed his cheek before she climbed from the car.

The idea came to Pierce in the early hours of the morning. As he tossed the light summer covers from his body and lay staring into the darkness he decided that he could not let Laine slip through his fingers. The kiss on the cheek had been a small step but a step at least. He knew he was right in thinking that underneath her chilly exterior lay a warm heart.

He rested his arms on the pillow above his head. There was no denying she had got under his skin. There was no point in trying to work out exactly when she had crept in. She just had. All he knew was that he had never felt this way before. And he suddenly realised he wasn't willing to let her walk away. Not without getting to know her a little better underneath that gorgeous armour.

It was just before three in the afternoon when he decided they could take a flight to Sydney to pick up what she needed for the shoot. The stores would be open on Saturday morning and they could call ahead and ensure everything was available. Then they could hire a car and drive to Toowoon Bay. His business manager could pull some strings and secure a villa for each of them at a beach hideaway for the weekend. It was a five-star resort, with stunning views over the South Pacific Ocean and the perfect getaway. They could stay

Saturday and Sunday night. The practice was closed from Saturday until Tuesday morning so Uralla didn't need him and James was in excellent care in the New England District Hospital.

There would be uninterrupted time for Laine to relax with him. To get to know each other and see where it took them. Or at the very least he would have a fascinating and beautiful companion for the weekend.

They would have some time to unwind and maybe, just maybe she would let down those walls and he would get to know more about this stunning and aloof woman. For the woman who was consuming most of his waking moments was now disturbing his sleep. He pictured her beautiful face, her soft lips and her deep green eyes like emerald pools that seemed to harbour sadness but still drew him in. She knew a little about him—perhaps not everything but enough—and while he knew even less about her, Laine had captivated him in a way that he'd never thought possible. He didn't want to live with the regret of never knowing what might have been.

He had dated a number of women over the years. Some relationships had lasted longer than others but none had been overly intense. They had been pleasant but there had always been something missing. But now there was this woman, who had forced him up a ladder, stood him up for dinner, sprayed him with oil in a paddock before the sun had warmed the air, had returned his kiss with an unbridled passion that he couldn't forget—and he wanted to see what lay beneath her cool exterior.

'I'm not sure.' Laine stood in the doorway to her room dressed in denim shorts, a white halter-neck top and sandshoes, with doubt evident on her freshly scrubbed face. She had listened sceptically to Pierce propose his plan for the two of them to fly to Sydney.

'Well, if you can think of a better way, be my guest,' he countered. 'But if you rely on a courier, then the equipment may not arrive here until late Tuesday. And that's still not a definite. You might be stuck waiting until Wednesday.'

Laine thought about what he was saying. She couldn't afford to wait that long. 'I suppose it's the only way really for me to meet my deadlines and be back in New York next week,' she admitted.

Pierce hoped she would accept his invitation and they would spend time together. Despite the fact they'd only just met, he knew he was developing feelings for this complex, at times exasperating woman. He sensed inside her lay a heart of gold that had been broken more than once. He thought they weren't that different. Each had something in their past that they wanted to forget.

Whatever she was hiding or running from drove her to live in the fast lane.

His past had seen him abandon the fast lane and live in a quiet country town.

But he sensed they both wanted to leave something behind. Maybe they could do it together.

'We can fly up there, pick up the replacement equipment and stay a couple of days to unwind. I'm sure after the schedule you've had with this calendar shoot that wouldn't be a bad idea. Speaking from a purely medical standpoint, you need to rest and recharge sometimes. Now is as good a time as any. The bank won't be open until Tuesday, but you can shoot first thing and be on a plane back to the States by lunchtime,' he reassured her.

Laine eyed the man standing at her door. She was very confused. And it wasn't just his suggestion of the brief holiday by the sea that was confusing her. It was the feeling in the pit of her stomach whenever he was near her and now was one of those times. She didn't want to feel anything for this man. Knowing more about him now was making it harder to not feel anything.

He was so wrong for her, or, more truthfully, she thought, she was wrong for him. A wife and a family would more than likely be in this country hero's plans and Laine could never be that woman. Perhaps she was overreacting to his invitation. Maybe it was a purposeful trip to collect her gear and then have some harmless R and R, but what if it wasn't? She couldn't allow herself to feel something, anything, for this man. It wouldn't work and even if it did, it wouldn't last. Love didn't.

'Okay, I'm sensing you need time to think about it,' he said, breaking the silence between them. 'What about we head over to the car-hire company and report the damage and they can send someone to pick it up then we drive into Armidale, visit the camera shop and see if they will need to ship in anything and how long it could take. Then, armed with that knowledge, you can make your decision. And if we need to head to Sydney, I'll get my travel agent to do it this afternoon.'

Laine liked the new practical direction of his conversation. His almost businesslike suggestion made it easier to breathe. The thought of a weekend away with Pierce was making her feel uncomfortable. And that was her problem, not his, she knew. It would be so easy to enjoy a fling, she had done it before and no doubt so had he, but for some reason she doubted she would walk away as easily from Pierce as she had from the others. This man had the kind of heart and soul she had not witnessed in a very long time.

'How about you get your things and we head off?'

Laine nodded and took a deep breath, hoping they could keep it casual. Sort out the car, pick up some equipment and forget the idea of sharing any more time than necessary with a man who was making her feel more than a little special.

'Okay…I'll grab my purse.'

With just under two hours until the first afternoon patient arrived at the practice, they climbed into the four-wheel drive and Pierce steered away the topic from Sydney and gave Laine an update on the young man now in ICU in Tamworth.

'He survived the night and according to the resident his chances of a full recovery are around seventy per cent. But he was driving unlicensed, under the influence of alcohol and he's only fifteen. Children's services have been brought in. He's fostered and the family have asked for help.'

'So they're not abandoning him?' she asked incredulously.

Pierce shook his head. 'No, apparently they want to get him counselling so he'll get on the straight and narrow. He's only been with them for a few months. His last placement was in Sydney and that family let him run amok so his new family wants to pull him into line and help him. He's had a bad trot with quite a few placements, the resident told me. Must have been rough on the poor kid and he fell in with a bad crowd and acted up.'

Laine rested back into her seat with a smile. 'That's

the best news. He's found someone who cares enough to ride out the bad stuff. He's fortunate, very fortunate,' she said. 'I just hope he appreciates what he has now. He's got to let go of the past and let them help.'

Pierce couldn't help but notice the emotion in her voice. Her work with the fostering charity was heartfelt. She was clearly a caring person with an obvious soft spot for children. There was little doubt in his mind that she was alone in the world by choice. But why she had made that choice confused him.

There was quite a lot about Jade that confused Pierce but even more that intrigued him.

'Do you want to have a family one day?' she suddenly asked. The discussion about the young man's new foster-family spurred her line of questioning. Family had meant nothing to Laine growing up and then it meant everything for a short while. Now she tried not to think about it.

'I suppose,' he replied, with his eyes on the road ahead. 'But I'm not in a hurry. What about you?'

'No,' she sighed as she looked out of the car window, her thoughts blurring the landscape. 'It's not for me but I'm sure you will.'

The tone of her response was not lost on Pierce. It was resolute with an underlying sadness.

Pierce didn't answer. He suspected she was right. He hadn't planned on it but deep down he knew he would love to come home to a family every night. His home had a yard big enough for a cubby house and a swing, even a dog. But he hadn't found a woman he had wanted to be with for ever. The woman he wanted to marry and be the mother of his children.

They headed to the car-hire company and explained

the incident and arranged for a replacement vehicle to be delivered to her motel. Pierce planned on dropping Laine at the camera shop while he checked on James in the New England District Hospital only a few streets away.

'I know you have my phone number but I don't have yours,' he told her, handing her his mobile phone. 'If I'm going to leave you at the store, can you put your number in my phone so I can reach you if I'm delayed?'

'Sure,' she said, taking the phone and quickly entering her details before she slipped it back on the console between them.

Pierce pulled up not far from the camera store and said he would be back in an hour.

The store stocked most of Laine's needs and the staff were very helpful. They made some calls and informed her that if she chose not to travel to Sydney they could have the lenses she needed couriered in some time on Tuesday. Taking their business card, Laine headed down the main street, still unsure what to do. She really wanted to do the shoot first thing Tuesday morning and fly off by lunchtime but that would mean travelling with Pierce.

Confused about the decision she had to make, she walked around the shops. She had visited Armidale as a teenager a few times and her memories of it were with wide eyes like Christmas morning. Now, compared to New York, she realised it wasn't the big city she once imagined. It was a lovely town, clean and pretty, but when she'd been growing up it had seemed like a metropolis to her. The stores had seemed so large and the streets so busy, and it had been a treat to make a trip there. Nothing like the quiet town she called home.

Now, all these years later, she appreciated the town for its relaxed ambience. No hustle and bustle, no tooting horns and mad foot traffic jostling each other for space on the kerb.

Finding an alfresco café, she sat down and closed her eyes for a moment and rested back in her chair. It surprised her how content she suddenly felt as she sat in the gentle warmth of the summer day, sipping her cool drink. The pace was so far removed from her usual life. She was eight thousand miles from her real home but suddenly she didn't miss it. She ordered an iced coffee and while she waited she reached into her purse for the business card and called the store.

'There's no need to bring in the lenses,' she told them. 'I'll pick them up in Sydney,'

She had done it. It was too late to turn back. The lenses could have arrived in time and she knew it.

She had made a decision to spend time with a man she liked. A man she admired.

The hospital visit was not as straightforward as Pierce had believed it would be.

Pierce arrived at the hospital to find that James had been transferred to Paediatric ICU.

'James unfortunately needed to be placed on a ventilator this morning. The oxygen therapy was failing him and his heart rate was falling. He also wasn't breast-feeding any more so he's on an IV to replace fluids,' Dr Myles Oliver, the paediatric consultant, told Pierce as they entered ICU together.

'How severe was the bradycardia?'

'Around fifty bpm while he sleeps,' Myles replied, as he checked the computer screen near the infant. 'But now we have the added issue of ventilation as little James's cough is compromising the pressure of the ventilator.'

'Is his mother aware of the complications?' Pierce asked, as he looked down at the infant unknowingly fighting the machine that was trying to keep him alive.

'She does know, and she's been great. Carla spent last night on a rollaway in the ward with James but now he's in ICU she'll be away from him when she sleeps.'

'If she sleeps,' Pierce replied.

'No, we will insist she leaves for a few hours' rest during the night. One of the nurses is walking with her to get a coffee now. She can't sit for hours without a break. It's not good for her or James if she's going without rest.'

Pierce watched as the ICU nurse gently stroked the child's arm as she checked the IV line.

'Honest prognosis?'

'James is an otherwise healthy baby. No issues with his health prior to this so we should be okay. We've had babies younger and less robust pull through, so without any further setbacks James will be fine. Although he'll be in hospital for a good month or so.'

'And you'll do a brain scan before discharging him.'

Myles walked with James to the door and out into the corridor. 'Yes, we'll be checking for any brain damage caused by the repeated low oxygen levels but I'm hopeful there won't be any problems if we can maintain ventilation. Great diagnosis, Pierce. The family knows that you got him here just in time.'

Pierce also checked if there had been any DUI admissions in A and E, but apparently not. The other youths had somehow passed through Armidale without incident. Their younger buddy had not been so lucky but hopefully he would leave that pack and turn his life around.

It was just over an hour before he called Laine, picked her up and they headed back down the highway to Uralla.

'I guess there's not a lot I can do in my room for three days, waiting for the equipment to arrive, and if it's not correct or gets mislaid then my next assignment in Rome will be compromised,' Laine said, looking straight ahead and trying not to make too much out of her announcement. It was logical and good business sense to fly away with Pierce. That was what she was telling herself, but inside she knew there was something more to it. Or rather someone who was making her want to take the trip.

'So you're accepting my invitation?'

'Sure, why not?' She knew she had all night to think it over and if she had a change of heart she would call and cancel and make do with the equipment she had purchased. It lessened the pressure. 'But I want to pay for my ticket. I'll write you a cheque or give you the cash. You're not paying for me.'

He could charter a plane to take her to Sydney without blinking an eye, but she wanted to pay her own fare. Pierce smiled at the gesture but he would not accept her money.

'How about you leave the air fares and accommodation to me, and you can buy lunch instead in Sydney? I like double ham on my sandwich so maybe I'll come out on top in this deal.'

After the serious but expected prognosis of his patient, this news lifted his spirits. He was still cautiously elated as he knew Laine had all night to think it over and perhaps get cold feet and change her mind. Although he hoped she just went with it and they had three days alone together. No cameras. No timelines. Just time by the sea with a beautiful and captivating woman.

'I'll pick you up around nine,' Pierce said as he dropped Laine at her motel door.

With her stomach starting to knot with apprehension, Laine took a deep breath and hesitated a little.

'Or perhaps ten's better?' he asked.

'No, no, nine's fine.' Laine was feeling so mixed up. She didn't know her own mind and she always knew and said what she wanted to. Now her emotions were suddenly in turmoil. A handsome man who she clearly found attractive wanted to spend time with her and she was feeling the same way and for some crazy reason she was as scared as hell. If this had been New York, she would run with it. Accept it for what it was. A few days of fun and nothing more. But Pierce was different. This town was different. And suddenly Laine felt different. And more than a little scared.

Pierce sensed she was feeling uncomfortable and he wanted to allay her fears. 'It's a great place. You'll enjoy yourself, just sun and beach and maybe a margarita or two.'

Laine swallowed the lump that had formed in her throat. It was hardly torture. Three days away with a handsome, kind and well-mannered bachelor. It seemed ludicrous to have doubts, but she did, serious doubts. Her barriers were unravelling a little more each minute she spent with Pierce. If she could just keep him at bay and keep herself in check it would be fine. There could be no fling. That was not negotiable. She spied him from the corner of her eye. Too damn good looking and she had the distinct feeling that it would take every ounce of her self-control not to be tempted.

'Okay, see you at nine,' she said, turning to go into her room. 'Unless something suddenly comes up.'

Pierce nodded. At least it wasn't a refusal but she had certainly kept the door open for a quick escape.

'See you at nine.'

Pierce arrived at eight-fifty the next morning and drove slowly down the motel driveway towards Laine's room. He felt apprehensive. The possibility that Laine might still cancel their trip away together weighed heavily on his mind. The fact that it did made him realise this woman meant more than any woman had ever done, particularly in such a short period of time. He knew it was crazy as she would never stay long term but he still wanted to spend time with her. It had been only a few days and yet he felt a connection that he wanted to explore on every level. Toowoon Bay would provide the perfect setting.

He pulled the four-wheel drive up to her door. His watch said five minutes to nine, so he decided to wait in the car for a few moments. He didn't want to arrive early or call to find Laine wasn't ready and give her a reason to decline the trip. He had no intention of coercing her into going away but he sensed part of her wanted to spend time with him too. Although, equally, there was also something that was holding her back. Something making her almost suspicious of him and not wanting to acknowledge she might be interested in getting to know him a little better too. Pierce wasn't sure what had caused Laine to build these walls around herself, but he wanted to try to break them down, just enough to see the real Laine. Maybe the sun would melt them, or the surf would wash them away. Or maybe he could peel them away.

Laine saw Pierce's car drive up to her door. She had spent the last hour sitting on the side of her unmade bed in cargo pants, sneakers and a white T-shirt, with her hair loosely tied in a low plait, wondering why she had agreed to go away. Her overnight bag sat packed by the door. A beachside resort in January meant a bathing suit, sarong, shorts, two summer dresses and sandals. It easily fitted into a carry-on bag. She had packed the night before, knowing if she didn't then she would more than likely change her mind in the light of day. Pierce was a lovely man but she didn't want a man like him in her life. He would complicate it.

There was a knock at the door.

She dropped her head into her hands and drew in a deep breath, stood up and in bare feet crossed to the door. This was without doubt a huge mistake. The third mistake. The first had been coming to Uralla and the second had been leaving her equipment in the car to be stolen. Could it be third time lucky or would this trip just be another disaster? she wondered.

'You're nothing if not punctual,' she remarked as she opened the door.

'So is the national train service,' he replied, a little deflated by her cold greeting. He had thought the day before that she had dropped her guard a little but now it was up like Fort Knox again. 'I was hoping for something a little more enthusiastic.'

'Nice shirt,' she said nervously, as she silently wondered what she had done. Going away with Pierce now seemed like a very bad idea. It wasn't him, it was most definitely herself she didn't trust.

Pierce could tell she was anxious. She hadn't greeted him by cancelling the trip but he suspected she was close to doing so.

'Thanks,' he said, glancing down at the navy cotton shirt he wore untucked over his beige shorts and leather loafers. 'A Christmas gift from Tracy, my receptionist, although I suspect her son Ben may have chosen it, he's the fashion compass of the town.'

Laine was trying to listen but her mind was spinning and she was barely concentrating. She wanted so badly to find an excuse, any excuse to cancel, but she couldn't verbalise a reason to say no to the man at her door. Try as hard as she could, it just wouldn't materialise. And a tiny part buried deep inside didn't want to cancel because that same tiny part wanted to spend time with this very handsome, very charismatic and, at times, witty doctor. He was growing on her and that was unnerving. She just wished she could block out that minority party in her head that was willing her to go away with him. She knew that no good would come of it. Now or later, if she even came close to falling for him, she would be hurt, that was certain.

'Well, I'm packed,' she said matter-of-factly, looking down at the overnight bag by the door.

Her tone and expression, similar to that of a woman heading to the gallows, did not go unnoticed by Pierce.

'If you don't want to go, just say the word. I can fly there, collect your gear and bring it back with me.' Pierce stepped back from the door and headed to his car. He wasn't about to force her to go. If she wanted

to spend time with him, the invitation was there. If not
then he would have a nice, albeit lonely weekend at the
resort. At the very least he was sure he would enjoy a
margarita by his private pool.

Laine realised that she had been less than gracious.
Pierce was just being friendly and she was behaving
poorly. Her problems should not be his. He wasn't asking for anything more than company for a few days.
For her it would be a weekend with no deadlines, no
clients, no temperamental models and apparently no
strings attached. She realised she was making more
of it than she should. Maybe it was all in her head. Or,
more precisely, all in her heart.

'I'm sorry,' she called to him. 'I guess the equipment
being stolen and the timeframe being thrown into disar-
ray has played on my nerves. But that's no excuse. Who
knows, a trip to the coast might be just what I need.'

Pierce paused in his tracks. 'No need to be sorry.
You've had a rough couple of days and there's no hard
feelings if you would rather stay in your room for three
days of lonely editing, only stepping out for food and
water.'

Laine smiled. She reasoned that few, if any, women
would refuse a weekend away with such a charming
man. 'No, you're not forcing me and I like the sound of
margaritas after the last few days I've had.'

Pierce looked long and hard at Laine. She was the
most complex woman he had ever met but he felt sure
if she ever allowed him to truly know her, his effort
would be rewarded tenfold.

'Then let's get out of here and get to the airport. Our
flight is in about fifty minutes. Time for a temporary
sea change.'

Pierce crossed back to her door and leaned in so close that she could smell the freshness of his still-damp hair from the shower and his woody cologne. Her pulse raced as her senses were filled with his masculinity, so near to her. He reached down for her bag and as he picked it up, his face swept dangerously close to hers. His soft lips were parted in a smile and she remembered vividly the tenderness that his kiss held.

She coughed nervously to pull her emotions into line. She felt overwhelmed but knew it was not his problem. There was so much tugging at her, so many feelings she'd left in this town and then there was Pierce, the last straw. She thought she might need that margarita sooner rather than later.

'So how long is this road trip after we finish our business in Sydney?'

'About an hour north,' he replied, as he opened the back door and placed her bag on the seat. 'Great scenery on the way, and the view the resort is spectacular.'

'Sounds good to me,' Laine said with a little sigh. Her feelings about the trip were not all that clear-cut but she intended on keeping it all to herself. Lifting the long strap of her handbag, she rested it on her shoulder and pulled the motel door closed. 'Let's go, then,' she said, as she climbed into his car and slipped on her oversized sunglasses. Pierce closed her door once she was safely inside, walked around to the driver's door and climbed in.

In no time they were at the airport, had checked in and were taking their seats on the forty-seater aircraft.

Laine buckled her seatbelt and made herself comfortable for the forty-five-minute flight. Briefly she looked out across the tarmac then turned to Pierce.

'So you can tell me to mind my own business, but what made you choose Uralla? I mean it's pretty much in the middle of nowhere and from what you said before, you lived in New York or at least spent some time there.'

Laine wasn't sure if Pierce would tell her the rest of his story or even part of it but she was hoping to hear just enough to remind her of their differences and throw any romantic overtones out the window before they took off. His desire to spend his life in a country town she hoped would send her heart back where it belonged. Tucked away from her lovely but all too perfect companion. She would for ever be a big-city dweller, at least that's what she told herself.

'I heard by word of mouth that there was the opportunity to be a partner in a country medical practice in a beautiful part of Australia and eventually buy out the retiring doctor so I thought, Why not? No traffic jams, no pollution and fresh eggs. Seemed like a great idea.'

He didn't want to spend more time discussing the family dynasty, money and scandal. He had left it behind and had never been happier. Now Pierce Beaumont was just a country practitioner with a real estate and investment portfolio that would anonymously support a great many causes indefinitely, and that was the only connection he had left to his family.

'I spent some time travelling as a child but I prefer this part of the world and I like to focus on the future. The analogy that the windscreen is so much bigger than the rear-view mirror is a valid one.'

Laine nodded in agreement. 'Isn't that the truth?'

For a moment they both looked out the small window in silence, each trying to forget something.

The plane had taken off on time and the landing was also on schedule. Pierce hired a car at the airport and headed to the camera store in the heart of the city. Laine had called ahead and said she would be collecting the lenses in person so they were ready when she arrived. Pierce watched as she walked around like a child in a candy store, looking at all the equipment. He could almost hear her squeal when she spotted a small sports camera she had been wanting and that too was packaged up with the lenses.

'You seem pretty chuffed,' he commented, as he took the heavy bag from the counter while she put her credit card back in her purse.

'Ecstatic, actually.'

Pierce was overjoyed to see Laine so happy. He wasn't sure why but seeing her smile made him just as happy. He didn't need another reason.

CHAPTER EIGHT

'MADAM'S MARGARITA, AS promised, and I took the liberty, considering the weather, of ordering the frozen variety.'

Laine smiled as she accepted the icy drink from Pierce. 'Perfect.' She sipped the salty, lime-flavoured cocktail and lay back on the sun lounge, looking through the palms to the holidaymakers on the beach, enjoying the perfect summer day.

They had pulled into the beachside resort an hour before and, just as Pierce had promised, they had separate accommodation. Laine felt guilty having asked for separate rooms when she found on check-in that he had booked her a spacious beach spa villa complete with private pool and sauna.

'I can't let you cover this, it's much too extravagant,' she told him.

'I insist. Besides, it was my idea, I needed a getaway weekend. Heading to Sydney to purchase your gear gave me the perfect excuse. It's nice to splurge now and then,' he said with a wink.

Laine graciously accepted but was relieved to discover his villa wasn't next to hers. No chance he would knock on her door in the middle of the night…and no chance she would impulsively knock on his either. She unpacked, changed into her red one-piece bathing suit and tied a sunset-coloured sarong around her hips before she made her way barefoot to the bar to meet Pierce.

'I agree, absolutely perfect,' he replied, but his remark was not in any way related to the drink. He was referring to the stunning brunette on the bar stool next to him. The open drape of the sarong exposed her long, honey-coloured legs, the scarlet swimsuit was cut low at the back and, at the front, shoestring straps held the plunging neckline in place.

Without doubt, Laine was the most gorgeous woman at the resort in Pierce's opinion and he didn't need to see another woman to know that was the truth. In his eyes she was by far the most gorgeous woman on the planet. Her body was lightly tanned, toned and healthy, her cleavage was small and appeared to be natural, which Pierce found even more appealing. Pierce found every inch of her body desirable. He could only imagine the parts not on display.

'I still can't believe I have my own pool, Pierce. Don't you think that's a little over the top?'

'Not at all. You need time out and you have it. Besides, you can always ask me to keep you company if you don't like swimming alone.'

Laine smiled. That was not the only pleasurable activity that they could share in her villa but she knew she wouldn't act on that thought.

'Do you surf?' she asked quickly, to change her thought pattern, as she looked out at the spectacular vista of beach stretched out before them.

'A little but I couldn't call myself a surfer.'

'So maybe we should stick to the shallows for a swim, then.' Laine looked across the crystal-clear water. It was enticing and the idea of swimming with Pierce in full view of the other guests made her feel safe. She didn't feel secure enough about her own feelings to swim in the villa pool alone with him.

'I don't claim to be a great surfer but we can venture into the ocean. I won't let you drown,' he replied, taking another sip of his drink. 'You can depend on me.'

Laine smiled in response. She had no doubt she could depend on Pierce but she never would.

The afternoon passed as they chatted about the resort over a light lunch, more talk about the stunning view of the beach and ocean, and even discovering that they had a mutual love of country music. Each claimed to have been a fan for longer, before they moved on to discussing Laine's return to the New York winter for two weeks and then her next shoot in Rome. Pierce suggested a swim. The water was perfect, initially a little cool against their warm skin as they plunged in but wonderfully refreshing.

Still lapping in the shallows at a leisurely pace, Laine watched as Pierce finally climbed from the water, his body glistening. His broad shoulders were tanned, his chest and torso were defined and muscular and, if possible, he looked even better soaking wet. He was drop-dead gorgeous. No debate about that. He ran his fingers through his thick black hair, walked over to the sun lounges they had claimed earlier on and, slipping on his sunglasses, lay down on the thick beach towel. There was no need to dry his body, the sun would do that quickly enough.

* * *

'I think you're blocking my sun,' Pierce remarked a few minutes later as Laine stood beside his lounge, slipping on her sarong.

'Pardon me,' she replied. '*Your sun?* How remiss of me not to watch where I was standing. I wouldn't want to cause you to have tan lines, now, would I?'

Looking up at the woman standing over him, Pierce wanted more than anything to pull her still-damp body onto his. To taste the sweetness of her mouth and then carry her to his villa and make love to her for the remainder of the afternoon and into the night. But that would never happen, she had made it clear enough. He had to get those images out of his mind. Still, he could enjoy the time he had with his stunning companion even if it was on her platonic terms.

'Well, if you agree to have dinner with me I'll forgive you.'

Laine laughed as she lay down on her sun lounge and slipped on her straw hat. 'I think I can manage that but not for a while yet. The sun is glorious and I have no intention of leaving here any time soon. I'll be knee deep in snow this time next week. Let me enjoy the sun while I can.'

'No argument from me. Let me know when you're hungry and until then I shall take an afternoon siesta.'

Laine worried that her sunscreen would have washed off in the water and reached into her bag, retrieved the lotion and, emptying some into her hand, began covering her exposed skin. Pierce watched from the corner of his eye as she stretched down and gently rubbed the sunscreen onto her legs and then her cleavage.

'Before I fall asleep, and you burn to a crisp, why

don't you turn over and let me cover your shoulders and back,' he said, as he gently claimed the bottle from her hand.

Laine smiled nervously. The thought of his hands on her body was an incredibly unsettling thought. Her stomach fluttered a little and she felt her pulse race, although he hadn't done anything more than brush his hand against hers when he'd moved over to her lounge and sat down beside her.

'Thank you...' she began, then faltered as the dampness of his swimsuit felt cool against her bare skin and his hands moved slowly over her shoulders without warning. In unison, like two skilled dancers, his hands travelled lightly across her skin with the lotion then moved slowly down both her arms.

The warmth of his touch made her breathing a little staggered. The movements of his fingers on her skin made her feel light-headed as they traced their way up and down her arms and then travelled to her bare back. Suddenly the pleasure she was feeling abated as he reached for more sunscreen. She hated that she wanted to feel his touch again.

Closing her eyes, Laine was grateful she was facing away from him and didn't have to mask her smile as his hands returned to her body and he began covering her back with the now-warm lotion. Trickles ran down the curve of her spine and his fingertips caught them before they disappeared beneath the fabric of her swimsuit. His hands worked their magic all over her back and then without warning he slid her flimsy sarong to the side and began working his way down the backs of her legs.

Not flinching was almost impossible as he massaged

her skin and slowly travelled down her thighs to the backs of her knees, where he paused for a moment, his lingering touch setting her skin on fire. Slowly he moved over the rise of her calves to her heels and then he gently worked the lotion into the soft, fleshy soles of her feet.

Laine kept her eyes closed and luxuriated in the feeling of his commanding hands on her bare skin. She couldn't remember ever feeling quite the way she felt at that moment. Her mind was floating, her body was more alive than it had ever been, and she was still partially dressed. His touch was intoxicating.

She was aware of every part of her body and could hear her own laboured breathing. She prayed he wouldn't stop.

'I think I've covered everything,' he announced, not wanting to stop or move away from her but realising he had no reason to stay. No reason that could justify keeping his hands on her body and feeling the softness of her skin or the warmth of her next to him for any longer.

Laine turned to face him. She looked up and softly thanked him before she turned away again. There was nothing else she could say. Although *Kiss me the way you did yesterday* was on the tip of her tongue, she knew she couldn't and she shouldn't. It wasn't right. Other than each having a past they would rather not discuss, they had little in common—in fact, they were miles apart, she told herself. And the following week they would be literally thousands of miles apart. It would never work. Despite their shared love of country music, they were two different people on very different paths in life.

Pierce closed the lid of the sunscreen, placing it

down near her bag, and then without saying another word he returned to his own seat. Although he was still only a few inches away, it felt like a gaping chasm. He wanted so much more.

With their minds fighting an avalanche of emotions, they both lay in silence. There was nothing Pierce could say and nothing Laine wanted to say. And so the afternoon passed with sunbathing and the occasional casual remark. Pierce found it difficult to mask the desire he felt for her so he avoided being that close again.

Laine wanted to forget the breathlessness she experienced as his hands had slowly roamed her body so she also played her part in their newfound distance from each other. Hours passed with the arrival of two other couples, their laughter filling the air as they too enjoyed the brilliant sun-drenched day. But there was an awkward silence between Pierce and Laine.

'I think I might head in for a shower before dinner,' Pierce announced unexpectedly, as he stood up and gathered his belongings.

'It's much too nice to leave yet,' she replied in a sleepy voice. 'I might stay a while and meet you later. What time did you want to eat?'

Pierce studied her for a moment then drew a long and purposeful breath before he answered. He was frustrated beyond belief at the situation and his tone was abrupt. 'I don't mind. Perhaps I'll come back down here when I'm ready. You can always stay in your swimsuit for dinner.'

'Then if we don't need to change, why don't you stay a little longer, too?'

Because I can't, Pierce thought. *Because being near you is driving me crazy.* He needed to get away from

Laine. She was more than just under his skin now. He knew if he had a cold shower and read a book it might help to snap him out of these ridiculous feelings. Something had to bring him to his senses and lying around with Laine in her barely-there bathing suit was not the solution. It was the problem.

'I think I've had enough sun for today.'

Laine watched Pierce walk away. It would have been so easy to reach out, take his hand and ask him to stay, but she knew better. He was a country doctor and she was not a fan of small towns any more, particularly the one he called home, so there was no point. In two days she would be leaving for her home in New York and Pierce would be the very kind and handsome man who graced the page of a calendar.

It was almost two hours before Pierce reappeared. He had showered and, in a still damp towel, lain on the freshly made bed, thinking about Laine. She was hauntingly beautiful but it was more than that. Pierce knew there was something in her past that was too painful to forget. She had obviously moved on, forged a life on her own, and a hugely successful life, but whatever had hurt her in the past was still there, driving her to be alone in the world. She was certainly an enigma and one he would not easily forget. But also not one he could solve.

He wondered if they were more alike than either of them imagined. Both wanted to move forward and never look back. But Laine seemed to take it one step further. Her journey forward seemed to be one she needed to do alone.

Later, dressed in white cotton shirt open at the neck and lightweight beige trousers with leather loafers, he took a stroll to the foyer bar to sit and enjoy a cool drink. The idea of sitting alone in his room was not appealing but sitting beside the object of his desire while she was sunbathing would be torturous.

The sun was almost ready to set and Laine had contemplated a few times making her way to her villa to change but had then decided, since she would be dressed in woollen leggings and a faux fur-lined parka in less than a week, she should make the most of the stunning summer weather. She also didn't want to be alone in the room with the object of her thoughts. Those thoughts had to be crushed. But finally, with no sign of Pierce and the sun showing signs of setting, Laine decided to head in to change for dinner after all.

She had a quick shower and slipped into an ankle-length white cotton sundress, flat gold sandals and pulled her hair into a high ponytail. Then she headed to the bar, suspecting that was where she might find Pierce. The fun-filled ambience had shifted gear. It was now more subdued, with almost romantic overtones.

Pierce was sitting astride a stool, waiting for her. His white shirt was unbuttoned slightly and contrasted starkly with his tanned skin. It would have been impossible for her not to admit to herself just how breathtakingly good looking he was at that moment. He was the stuff that sold magazines, that covered billboards and broke hearts, and yet she knew at least two of the three were not close to what he did. She had no idea if he broke hearts and she had no intention of finding out.

'So you changed after all,' he said, as he watched her walk towards him. Her dress was thin cotton and it flowed around her, allowing him to make out the curves of her body with each step she took. It was low cut and he could see the outline of her perfect breasts. He felt certain there was nothing between her skin and the soft fabric.

She became more desirable with every passing second.

'Well, it would look a little odd if you're dressed and I'm in bathers.'

Pierce just smiled, a knowing kind of smile. He knew there would be no complaints from him or any other man in the restaurant if she had glided in with just a flimsy sarong over her scarlet swimsuit. None at all.

'So, are we ready to eat dinner?'

'Well, I am. Are you?'

Pierce led the way to the restaurant with huge glass windows, allowing panoramic views over the beach. The sun had almost set as they were directed by the *maître d'* to one of the tables near the windows. Wild orchids and tealights dressed the intimate table that was to be theirs for the evening. They were so close to the beach that the crashing of the waves on the shore could be heard over the low chatter of the other patrons.

Pierce pulled out Laine's chair and once she was seated he made his way to the other side of the table and sat down.

Laine looked out across the expanse of white sand now lit by the moon. 'It's so beautiful here. Truly, it's the perfect getaway. There's no reason to leave, everything we could possibly want is right here in front of us and it's stunning.'

Again Pierce didn't disagree. He knew that everything he could possibly want was right in front of him. She was stunning and he was doing his best not to entertain thoughts that she would never reciprocate.

'Pre-dinner drink?' the waiter asked, as he handed them the menus. Flicking open the large white fabric napkins, he placed one on Laine's lap and another on Pierce's.

'I think I'll have my second margarita. You promised me three and I've only had one since we arrived almost seven hours ago.'

'Then two margaritas, please,' Pierce requested, handing the wine list back to the waiter.

Laine and Pierce both studied a menu. Each menu was filled with such an array of fresh seafood dishes that they both found it difficult to decide. Their drinks arrived as they were trying to make a final choice.

'The Moreton Bay bug tails sound delicious, what about you?'

Pierce looked over the menu a little longer. 'Think I'll go with the lobster.'

Laine smiled as she took a sip of her drink. 'Looks like we have a mutual love of seafood, then.'

Pierce signalled the waiter and placed the order, adding some mixed tapas for an appetizer.

'Not sure I be able to fit it all in but I'll try,' Laine remarked softly, then turned to look across the now silver ocean. The moon was hovering in a crescent shape and lighting the ripples in the water. 'It's so beautiful. Thank you for inviting me.'

'You are very welcome.'

The tapas and dinner were delicious, with the fresh citrus flavour in the salads being the perfect partner to both seafood choices.

'Shall we take a stroll on the beach? It's such a beautiful night and it's still early.'

Pierce was surprised by Laine's suggestion but happy to oblige as he wiped his mouth on the napkin and stood up to leave.

'But you'll have to roll up your trousers and lose the shoes,' she added.

The sand was still warm as they finally stepped onto the beach in front of the restaurant. Lanterns lit the area softly and made it easy for them to find their way to the water. Eager to feel the cool water on her feet, Laine tied up the hem of her dress in a knot so she could splash in the shallows.

'I should probably swim along the coastline for about five miles after all that I ate,' she said, as she felt the cool water wash over her feet.

'Great idea. I think that after about one mile cramps would set in and then shortly after that you could possibly drown.'

She looked up to see Pierce smiling back at her. 'You're a doctor, so you can save me.'

Pierce walked away from the water's edge and sat down on the soft sand, dropping his loafers beside him. 'Might not find you in the water. It's pretty dark.'

Laine walked back up to where he was sitting and lay down beside him. Untying the knot in the hem, her flowing dress spread out over the soft waves of the sand.

'I think you would find me.'

Pierce silently agreed. He would find her. He wouldn't let anything happen to Laine. She was the toughest porcelain doll he had ever met, but he knew underneath she still was a porcelain doll. Fragile and precious under a hardened exterior.

'Do you want another drink at the bar or do I risk inducing an alcohol problem?'

'No, I've polished off my two margaritas and that will be my limit for the entire weekend, I think,' she replied, looking up at the moon. It was a perfect night. The air was fresh but it was still warm enough to sit by the water and her companion suddenly became appealing on a level she'd never expected.

'Okay, no drink. What about a long walk or—?'

'How about we watch a movie?' She cut his line of questioning short. 'I'm sure they'd have cable or pay-per-view here, so why don't we watch an old movie?'

Watching old movies had been something she'd done with her adoptive parents. To many it would seem normal, growing up watching television with the family, but in many of her foster-homes it had been rare or non-existent. She would be sent to her room as they wanted to watch their choice of programme and claimed it wasn't suitable for a child. She would be alone or sharing with a foster-sibling who was equally unhappy and they would hear the adults in another room, laughing and enjoying television, while they sat in the dark. She had always hoped one day to be a part of a family who included her, and when it had finally happened it had been as much fun as she had imagined. Sitting together, sharing a movie and popcorn, was a joy. Now she wanted to share that with Pierce.

'Sounds great.' Pierce wasn't sure where this would lead but he also wouldn't refuse the opportunity to spend time with Laine. He had tried to stay away that afternoon but now, this close, he knew he would agree to pretty much anything she suggested.

'It's still early and if we stay out here eventually the mosquitoes will find us.'

Pierce stood and reached down for Laine's hand and pulled her up on her feet. 'A black and white movie it is, then.'

'Let's see if there's one that neither of us has seen,' she said, as her feet disappeared in to the soft sand and she again needed to lift up the hem of her dress as they walked back to the restaurant.

Laine made herself comfortable in a large armchair in the corner of the room and kicked off her sandals.

'That's not about to happen,' Pierce said, as he walked into the room with some iced water and found Laine huddled in the chair. 'Let me take the chair and you can make yourself comfy on the bed.'

'Are you sure?'

'I insist.'

'Always the gentleman.'

'Not always,' he muttered, as he reached for the remote control and found the movie channel on his way to the armchair. He, too, kicked off his shoes and made himself comfortable as Laine climbed onto the bed and fluffed up the pillows behind her back, before nestling into them. The ceiling fan above gently moved the warm evening air about the room.

As he scrolled through the selection Laine finally caught sight of the movie she wanted. '*Detour*, with Ann Savage.'

'Never heard of it,' he announced.

'Great, that means you will always remember me sitting in your room and watching this film noir thriller for the first time.'

Pierce knew it wouldn't be the movie he would remember. He would remember everything about Laine,
more than she could possibly imagine.

'You seem to know all about it. If you've seen it then
we should select something else. You said you wanted
to see a movie that neither of us had seen.'

'I did and I meant it. I haven't seen this movie but I
always wanted to. It was produced by a small studio in
the mid-forties, it was low budget and they called the
studio one of the poverty-row studios because they had
so little money. But it's a classic.'

'If you say so,' he said, resting back into his chair
as the movie started.

It was not only a long movie by most standards but
Pierce noticed Laine fall asleep about thirty minutes
into the film. He crossed the room and placed a lightweight blanket over her then went back to his chair. He
worried that if the temperature dropped and there was
an ocean breeze she might get cold during the night.
With no conversation likely, Pierce watched the movie
until the end while still keeping a watchful his eye on
his sleeping guest. It felt good to have her near. The
fact she was asleep didn't matter. She was close and
he was happy.

He finally dimmed the lights and brought a chair
from the desk alongside his armchair and stretched out.
It wasn't the most comfortable of beds but it would do.
He looked over at Laine. Her face looked so angelic
as she slept, almost looked as if she were smiling. He
drifted off to sleep wondering if she was dreaming and
whether he featured within her thoughts.

Laine woke to see Pierce sleeping upright in the

chair. 'You let me have the bed and you slept like that?' she said softly as she tapped his shoulder. 'You can't do that. I have a whole villa to myself and I'm taking your bed.'

Still drowsy, Pierce looked over at Laine. 'I'm fine, go back to sleep. Honestly, you need the rest.'

'That is taking chivalry to the extreme, actually the ridiculous,' she stated, sitting upright and trying to untangle her bed hair with her fingers. 'I'll leave, and you can get some sleep in your very expensive bed and I will go back to my equally expensive sleeping quarters.' She lifted her legs and swung around to find her shoes in the dim light.

'Your villa isn't next door,' he reminded her. 'You're across the other side of the resort. So stay here until morning. You're doing me a favour by staying. If you leave I will have to walk you all the way over there and then come back.'

'I'm a big girl. I'm pretty good at taking care of myself. Don't forget I live in New York so I think I can make a three-minute walk at...' She paused, looking unsuccessfully for a clock. 'Whatever time it is now.'

'Fine, be stubborn, but I'm walking you there.'

Laine reached inside her purse and discovered the swipe card for her room was missing, and quickly realised it was in her beach bag, not her purse.

'I can't believe it...'

'Can't believe what?' he cut in.

'My room card, it's in my other bag. The one I had with me when I was sunbathing. I'm guessing the front desk is closed at this ungodly hour.'

'Yes, I'm pretty sure you'd be right about that.'

'So now what am I going to do?'

'I think the universe has pretty much decided it for you.'

Laine knew he was right and she also knew that few women would be upset by the prospect of a night in the room of an eligible bachelor with the sex appeal of Pierce. But Laine was already struggling to keep their relationship platonic without staying the night with him. But now she had no choice.

'Fine, I'll stay. But you can't spend the rest of the night in that chair. We do have a king-size bed,' she said, swallowing her nerves. 'I think we can manage to share it for a few hours.'

'I'm okay here. When I asked you to stay the night, I wasn't asking to sleep with you.'

'Don't you think I know that? If you were expecting me to *sleep* with you, I'd be leaving now even if I had to sleep in the foyer. But you have paid an exorbitant amount for two villas for us, and it's not your fault I forgot my room key, so I absolutely won't let you sleep on a chair.'

Pierce smiled. 'How can I refuse such a gracious invitation?' He made his way over to the other side of the bed in silence. He stripped off his trousers and un-buttoned his shirt, throwing it across to the desk and, wearing only his tight-fitting black boxers, he slipped into the bed beside Laine.

Not admitting she had watched him remove his clothing, and painfully aware that she had little under her dress, she softly said, 'I suppose I should do the same, otherwise my walk of shame in the morning will have the added embarrassment of having an incredibly creased dress.'

CHAPTER NINE

PIERCE WOKE IN the morning to a sight that made him smile. Laine was lying almost naked in his bed. His eyes appreciatively traced the curve of her spine as it disappeared under the covers. Her warm body was close to him but he knew he had no right to touch her. She had stayed because he asked her to do so, and he wasn't about to break the trust they were building by making a move in the light of morning. Although it took every ounce of self-control not to reach over and pull her into his arms and make love to her.

Moments later, Laine opened her eyes slowly, surveyed the room and immediately realised where she was. Sharing a bed with Pierce. Lying very still, she navigated the logistics of getting dressed without crossing the room naked to retrieve the dress that she had carefully draped over the armchair.

Unsure whether Pierce was still sleeping, she slowly turned in the bed, pulling the sheets with her to cover her breasts.

'Good morning, sleepyhead,' his husky voice breathed.

Laine was face to face with Pierce. Resting his head on bent arm, his dark, smouldering eyes were staring straight at her. His lips hovering very close to hers. Lips that only two days ago had kissed her so passionately. He was smiling and the dark stubble on his chiselled chin, now more pronounced, was shading his powerful jaw.

Laine gave a nervous cough. 'Good…morning.'

She drew the sheets more tightly around her. She wasn't scared of the man beside her, she was scared of her own desire. Inviting him to make love to her would be so easy but she knew it would put her at risk of being hurt. They would have to say goodbye in twenty-four hours and now, looking at him in the light of morning, she knew that would be painful. Now she actually cared. Life had dealt Pierce some hard blows and yet he had managed to stay afloat and not harden against the world. Just because he wasn't jaded, she had mistaken a genuinely grounded man for one who was privileged and spoilt by life.

'Would you like to take a swim to start the day?'

Laine could think of something she would prefer to do and was grateful that Pierce did not suggest it as she doubted she would be able to refuse. To stay wrapped in his strong arms, sharing his warm bed for the entire day would be heaven.

'Perfect,' she announced, pulling herself up in the bed, tugging the sheets with her as she moved away from his warm body. She struggled awkwardly to keep the sheet covering herself as she made her way to the edge.

A curious furrow deepened on his brow as Pierce realised her struggle. 'I'm going to hop in the shower while you manoeuvre yourself out of the oversized bandage you've made of our sheets.'

Our sheets. The words resonated with Laine. There had been no *our* anything for so many years. It had always just been hers. She hadn't shared anything since she'd left her family home. *Our* sounded wonderful but she knew even thinking like that was crazy. He was her travel companion, and she had to remind herself of that. There could never be *our* anything between them.

'Great,' she mumbled. 'I'll go to my room, do the same and meet you on the beach in fifteen.' Friendly plans. Perfect.

'Make it half an hour, it will take you fifteen minutes to find a way out of the strait-jacket you've created.' He laughed then climbed from the bed.

From the corner of her eye she spied his broad tanned shoulders in the early morning light. The muscles of his back were gently defined and the curve of his bottom was held firm in his tight-fitting black boxers. She pretended not to watch as he collected his belongings from his overnight bag and disappeared into the bathroom.

Laine waited to hear the water running before she undid the sheets and made her way to her dress and out of the door.

'Well, it didn't take you long to leave my room this morning,' Pierce began, as he stepped onto the sand. He was wearing the same navy swim trunks as the day before and carrying a towel and grinning as made his way to Laine, who was already lying in her red swimsuit on a beach towel. 'Not even a five-minute shower. I came out and there was no sign of you. You're quick.'

'I didn't want to waste a minute of the sun today,' she said, masking the real reason for her hasty exit. The idea of still lying in the warm bed when Pierce emerged from the bathroom with only a towel covering his wet body would have been too tempting for her.

But now, out in the sunlight, she was questioning if she should have given in to her desires after all. Her emotions were travelling like an out-of-control train and she had no idea where she was heading.

But it was a glorious day, and she intended to enjoy it.

Pierce dropped his towel beside her. 'Are you actually going to hit the water or just sit there all pretty on the beach?'

Laine glared at him. 'You're in so much trouble for that!'

Pierce hastily tucked his wallet, car keys and room card under the towel and raced to the water, with Laine in hot pursuit. His body disappeared beneath the waves before she reached the water's edge so she dived in after him. The water was crystal clear and Laine opened her eyes to see the stunning underwater world hidden to those on the sand. After a minute she rose to the surface, drew in a breath and submerged a little longer. On her second trip to the surface she found Pierce looking back at her.

'You constantly surprise me,' he confessed in a husky tone. 'I never thought of you like this. I thought New York may have taken the love of the great outdoors from you. But it hasn't so I guess I can't keep thinking of you as a prima donna now.'

'Me, a prima donna? First it's all *pretty on the beach* and now a *prima donna*! You're asking for trouble.' With her cupped palms full of salt water she playfully splashed his face before she swam off in the clear blue ocean.

Pierce wiped his face then swam in her direction. His powerful arms proved no match for her small strokes and he quickly caught up. 'Feisty in the mornings, aren't we?' he teased, as he swam alongside her.

Laine was so happy. The sun, the water, the man. The warmth and security she'd felt lying next to him in his bed. The trust she had found with a man she barely knew yet suddenly found she understood. It was starting to wash away a lot of her resentment about life Down Under. She didn't want to feel so carefree but she had no choice. Suddenly the Laine of the last twelve years was emerging from her lonely cocoon and spreading her wings. And it was all because of the man swimming beside her. Pierce was changing her game plan and she was helpless to stop him.

'I've booked a table for breakfast,' Pierce announced as they walked dripping from the shallows onto the sand and headed to their belongings. 'I thought we might be hungry after lapping the coastline.'

'Absolutely starving,' she said softly, rubbing her hair dry with her towel.

Pierce looked at the woman beside him and thought she appeared different, a little less on edge. More playful and relaxed than even the day before. Perhaps her walls were crumbling a little.

'Great, let's head up there now. We can sit outside under an umbrella in our swimsuits.'

Smiling they walked up to the alfresco section of the restaurant, placed their towels on their chairs and sat down in their still-damp swimsuits to order breakfast. Pierce soon learned that 'absolutely starving' for Laine did not extend to the bacon, eggs, grilled tomatoes on

toast with a cappuccino that he had chosen for himself.
Her order was Greek yogurt with a tropical summer
fruit selection, sparkling water and a long black coffee.

'In twenty years you'll have the better arteries but I
will have enjoyed my Sunday breakfasts far more, although you clearly have great genes and don't have to
worry anyway.'

Laine froze. Her look suddenly became serious and
she didn't respond in any way to his compliment for
a moment. No smile, no frown, nothing. Pierce was
confused. He wasn't sure what he'd said that could
suddenly dampen the otherwise great time they were
having.

'Somehow I just did it again,' he said sombrely. 'Believe me, it was a compliment. Your mother was no
doubt a beautiful woman.'

Laine looked into the warmth of his eyes. He had
no idea what he had said that could have upset her. He
deserved to know it wasn't him, it was the sadness of
her past still darkening the present.

'I never met my mother,' she said with a sigh as she
looked out across the blue horizon where the water met
the azure sky.

Pierce looked deep into her eyes and reached for her
hand. He didn't hesitate. It felt natural to comfort her.
'I'm so sorry. I didn't mean to upset you. It's the last
thing I would want to do.'

Laine's lips curled but her smile was tinged with
sadness. 'I know you didn't, Pierce.' She looked down
and saw his hand covering hers and she didn't want to
pull away. 'How were you to know your date for the
weekend was abandoned at birth? Born to people who

didn't want me or for some reason couldn't keep me, I'll never know.'

Laine was surprised it didn't hurt as much as she'd thought it would to say it. She'd never allowed the words to pass over her lips before and it wasn't as painful as she had imagined. Maybe she didn't care any more. Or perhaps it was the person listening who made it easier.

Pierce suddenly put the pieces together. 'So you became a foster-child. That's why you have an affinity with the charity?'

'Yes,' she said softly. 'I didn't have a particularly good time as a foster-child, way too many placements with families who didn't give a damn about me. Many foster-families are amazing, and many foster-children have wonderful lives, I know, but unfortunately I wasn't one of the lucky ones, well, not until the end. And by then, let's say the scars ran deep.'

Pierce looked at Laine with a newfound understanding. 'You're an amazing woman and you've achieved so much for having had such a sad childhood.' Pierce didn't pull his hand away. He wanted her to feel secure.

Laine continued, 'My final family, Maisey and Arthur, were the most loving people and they adopted me so they should take the credit for my success. I went to live with them in Uralla when I was twelve and they taught me what family really meant. I owe it to them to make the most of my life.'

He suddenly knew how she knew so much about the town. Everything fitted into place but he was aware there was still a lot of hurt and anguish she was carrying from her past. Although he wanted to know more about her upbringing, he did not want to cause her any further pain so instead he added, 'Well, they must be so proud of you...'

Laine hastily lifted her gaze to meet his and gently pulled her hand free. She didn't want him to know any more. To learn they had both died. She had already said too much. 'Enough about me. I wasn't twelve and left alone after being forced to jump from a burning building to save my life.'

'When you put it like that, it sounds dramatic. But we've both had quite rough trots in life and, hey, look at us now. We've done something right on our own, hey?'

'But surely you weren't on you own? You weren't even a teenager.' Laine took another spoonful of her yogurt and wiped her mouth with the cotton napkin.

'In a manner I suppose I was,' he replied, pausing to take the last bite of his meal. 'My father's much older sister, Mabel, was given custody in the will and she'd never married, let alone had children. Growing up, I hadn't seen much of her so we weren't close and she wasn't in the best of health. Whatever the real reason, she said she wouldn't be very good as a surrogate parent. She worried that a boy raised by his maiden aunt might miss out on a balanced upbringing so she sent me to boarding school overseas. In hindsight maybe it was a sensible decision but at twelve it was hard, suddenly being thrown on a plane to the other side of the world after losing my family.'

Laine shook her head in disbelief. 'That would have been terrible. You would have still been grieving.' She drew a breath and continued shaking her head. 'Now I'm not sure who had the worst childhood. Close contest really between you and me.'

'Mabel did what she thought was right. I guess we

can safely say we've survived the worst, so we will get through anything life can throw at us.'

'Maybe,' Laine said sombrely. 'Or perhaps we're so battle worn we won't survive the next heartbreak.'

Pierce looked at Laine for a moment and knew that her grave outlook on life was colouring everything else in it. 'You're an amazingly resilient woman and, who knows, perhaps the universe is done testing both of us and it'll be smooth sailing for the next sixty years.'

'Who knows…?'

Laine finished her sparkling water and looked out over the beach in silence.

Pierce noticed the distance in her eyes. Her pain was almost palpable and he didn't want her to start rebuilding the walls around her heart. He now understood her need to protect herself but he wanted her to feel safe with him. To be able to lose the need to be on the defensive and just enjoy their time together. He needed to turn the day around. Quickly.

'How about you and I head off for a nice drive to a place the concierge told me about this morning? It's a native animal and bird reserve and rainforest about thirty minutes from here called the Forest of Tranquillity. We can stay cool amongst all the greenery,' he said, standing and extending his hand to her.

Laine looked at his hand and then her gaze lifted to linger on the curves of his handsome smiling face for a moment. Then, surprising even herself, she reached up and rested her hand in his and her lips curved to a smile as she nodded.

Pierce was pleasantly surprised at her reaction. Perhaps there still was a chance for them. He wasn't sure what the chance would be but he wanted to explore whatever direction it took.

'Should I change?' she questioned him.

'Not a thing,' he told her, insisting that a sarong over her swimsuit was perfect attire for wherever they went, and pointed out that he was in swimming trunks too. He didn't bother with a T-shirt as the day was perfect and if the weather forecast was correct, in just a matter of hours it would be a scorching hot summer's day.

'It's a rainforest on the Australia Day long-weekend. It's not Park Avenue,' he said, opening the car door for her. 'Dress code around here on a one-hundred-degree day is "remain decent but no need to overdo it"!'

Laine laughed as he closed the car door. She could learn a lot from Pierce. He was good for her and she knew it. He put the past where it belonged. She hoped one day to be able to do the same. She just didn't know how long it would take.

The day passed quickly as they made their way around the rainforest sanctuary in the slowing rising temperature. They enjoyed an Australia Day celebration barbeque lunch before they headed off again on the forest walk.

'Let's do a spot of bird-watching,' Pierce said lightheartedly.

'Definitely haven't done that before,' she said, 'unless you count avoiding pigeons in Time Square.'

Pierce rolled his eyes. 'Then you are in for a treat, because you will witness over one hundred and twenty birds here.'

'Really, one hundred and twenty here today?'

'Well, you may have to spend a few weeks or maybe

months for them to all to return home but it says here,' he told her, pointing to the coloured brochure in his hand, 'that one hundred and twenty-six species of native birds have been recorded in the sanctuary.'

Laine playfully hit his shoulder. 'You're crazy...like one of those over-enthusiastic biology teachers.'

'Maybe I missed my calling,' he replied, as they sat down on a wooden bench under the shade of a tree. 'I could become a professional bird-watcher. I'd just need some binoculars and a safari suit. Now, that's a fashion statement that needs to be brought back. What do you think? With your fashion contacts, can you make it happen?'

Laine listened to his silly ramblings as she stretched her legs out in front of her and looked up at the perfect blue sky peeking through the dense greenery. Their surroundings were stunning.

'Unfortunately, not even my favourite fashion bible could resurrect that disaster. Besides, I'm not sure you have the patience required to wait for one hundred and twenty-six birds to return home.'

Pierce smiled. Perhaps not. But he did have the patience to wait for Laine to fall for him, he thought as he watched her suddenly jump to her feet with the arrival of a small yellow and grey plumed bird. She began to take photos with the new camera she had purchased in Sydney. The day was relaxing just as Pierce had hoped and he noticed Laine's mood lift, just as he had planned. Pierce smiled as he watched her face light up, waltzing around happily taking snaps of the birds in their natural habitat. He thought back over the last few days and how only week ago he hadn't even known the woman who had his complete attention now.

Laine turned around to see Pierce leaning against a low wall of uneven rocks. His suntanned chest was bare, his bathers hung low over his taut stomach and his gorgeous face was radiant with the most perfect smile. *Perhaps returning to Uralla and meeting Dr Pierce Beaumont wasn't a mistake, after all,* she thought to herself as she snapped his photo. Perhaps, for some reason, it was meant to be.

The day turned into evening and they chatted happily as they drove back to the resort with plans for a refreshing swim in the private pool in Pierce's villa before dinner.

They were alone in the secluded villa garden as the sun set.

'Thank you for a lovely day—in fact, two lovely days,' Laine said, as she sat on the pool's edge, dangling her feet in the water as she dried off in the warm evening breeze.

Pierce swam over to her and looked up into her beautiful smiling face. 'You are more than welcome but I should be the one thanking you for agreeing to join me.'

Laine looked down at his handsome warm face and realised the last two days she had spent with Pierce had melted the last of her reserves. Suddenly she didn't want to hold back any more. She slipped her still-wet body back into the water and into his arms. Without thinking, she kissed him. Then, feeling scared at what she had done, she pulled away.

Pierce pulled her back towards his hard body and

kissed her with the passion of a man possessed. His lips kissed hers with desire that he had never felt before. His hands caressed her body, sliding over her shoulders, teasing the straps of her swimsuit as he threatened to slip them off. Slowly she opened her mouth and kissed him with abandon. She wanted him too and she was not going to hold back. He pressed her against the pool edge as his hands slipped down the small of her back and rested on her bottom.

'I think we should take ourselves inside,' he breathed softly into her ear, and he kissed her neck.

Laine nodded and, holding her tiny waist, he lifted her from the water and placed her on the pool edge before he hauled himself up beside her. His tender kissed trailed across her shoulders and up her neck until he reached her eager mouth.

He had a look in his eyes that she felt in her heart.

Standing up, he reached down for her hand. Only this time he knew he wasn't offering a drive into town to distract her. They were about to become lovers. Laine willingly allowed him to pull her into his arms again. Strong, warm arms that she knew would hold her all night. Neither said anything as he scooped her up in his arms and carried her to the bed, their kisses becoming more intense with each step.

He wasn't waiting a second longer to have her. The room was lit only by the moonlight but it was enough for Pierce. He could see her beautiful sparkling eyes looking up at him as he slowly slipped her bathing suit from her body, kissing every part of her body as he inched the suit down. Finally he threw the swimsuit across the room, his own swimming trunks joining hers a moment later on the floor. Then his mouth slowly, purposefully began kissing his way up back her body again.

'Are you sure?' he asked huskily, as he slipped on the protection he had taken from his wallet.

Laine moaned her answer and pulled him to her. She was more than sure.

CHAPTER TEN

THEY LAY IN each other's arms for the longest time. Laine had floated to a place she never knew existed. She named it bliss in her head and hoped to visit again very soon. Pierce silently declared himself the luckiest man in the world. Both realised they were falling in love.

Pierce was not yet ready to tell Laine.

Laine was not yet ready to tell herself.

'Can I say, you're an amazing woman,' Pierce said, cupping her face in his hands and kissing her softly.

Laine kissed him back and pressed her body into the warmth of his embrace. His naked body felt so good next to her. Without doubt he had been the best lover—kind, considerate and passionate. Smiling to herself as she looked over his shoulder at the desk where, after throwing the contents of the desktop on the floor, he had made love to her, she added *surprisingly innovative* to the mental list.

'I definitely can't take all the credit for the last... how many hours?'

'Don't know, don't care,' he said, as his hands gently roamed her body and he listened for signs of her pleasure, lingering when he heard a response.

'I would love to continue this all night,' she murmured as his kisses moved slowly down her neck, 'but we might need to eat or they'll find two bodies in the morning, wearing big smiles but bodies none the less.'

Pierce smiled and lay back down on the pillow. 'Point taken.'

Laine rolled over to face him. 'I'm thinking that I rather like our state of dress, so what if we order room service then only one of us has to leave bed?'

Pierce replied as he looked at the woman who was closer than any woman had ever been to claiming his heart. Her long brown hair was trailing across the pillow, framing her smiling face, and the sheets were barely covering her body. There was none of her earlier modest sheet wrapping. 'And that *one* would be me?'

'Do you mind?'

Pierce climbed from the bed. 'Not at all, but I'll need some swim trunks and a menu.'

'I think they're both on the floor,' Laine told him with a grin. 'The menu was on the desk a few hours ago but it's definitely not there any more.'

'And the swim trunks were on me a few hours ago and they're definitely not any more either.' A wicked glint appeared in eye and he leant back down on the crumpled sheets and began kissing her again.

'I'm thinking grilled chicken salad,' she told him, as she gently pushed him away.

The order arrived a short time later. Pierce carried it to the bed as Laine emerged from the shower and sat down beside him in a towel with her hair up in a clasp.

'I'm so ridiculously hungry,' she began as she picked

up a fork and began selecting pieces of grilled chicken from the salad plate, ignoring the leafy mix and tomatoes.

'I think I know why,' he replied with a smirk as he cut into his steak.

Laine ignored his remark and continued eating. There was nothing left on her plate when she had finished. Not even a basil leaf. 'Do they have strawberries and cream on the menu?'

Pierce removed the tray from the bed and carefully placed it on the floor near the door. He slid over to Laine, pulled the clasp from her hair and slowly opened her towel, revealing her naked body to his appreciative eyes. 'Let's forget the strawberries, keep it simple and just order whipped cream.'

It was after midnight when they fell into a deep, satisfied sleep. Laine was secure in the strong arms that encircled her. Pierce held everything he knew he could possibly want in the world. The empty dessert bowls lay on the floor with the other dishes.

Pierce awoke in the morning as the sunlight crept through the blinds and spread across the bed. Laine was still in a deep sleep. The trip, he decided, had definitely been the best idea he had ever entertained. With careers on different continents, Pierce had no idea how their relationship would work but he decided then and there that he would make it happen somehow. Staring at the patterns the sunlight and blinds were making on the ceiling, he decided he would not give up easily.

Laine opened her eyes, in more ways than one.

She woke to realise the enormity of what she had

done. She had broken two rules in one night. She had slept with one of her *models* and she had slept with someone she cared about. Even worse, someone who cared about her.

It had the makings of a disaster...yet she had never been so happy in all her life.

Pierce noticed her stirring and, lifting the mass of messy brown locks away from her neck, gently began kissing her bare skin. The stubble on his chin was tickling her but the desire he stirred again overrode everything else. Gently he rolled her on her back and looked into her eyes. His gaze was intense, as if he was looking into her soul.

'You must know how I feel...I...'

Laine put her finger to his lips and then followed it with a kiss. She was scared he might say he was falling in love with her. She didn't want him to spoil it. Her own heart was saying it too and now she realised she wasn't ready to hear the words. She might *never* be ready to hear them. They lived on different continents, lived different lives. It was overwhelming to think that she could be falling in love. It could never happen.

As the sun hit his chiselled jaw, once again darkened by a fine covering of stubble, she told herself she had no choice but to accept they were like two ships who had collided for one amazing night.

Pierce pulled away. 'We can make this work. If you want to see where we can take it.'

Laine closed her eyes. 'Let's not—'

Suddenly the ringing of Pierce's mobile phone interrupted her answer.

'Now, that's got to be worst timing,' he muttered in an irritated tone as he reached down to find it on the floor. Immediately he knew the caller from the screen. 'Hello, Tracy, what's happened?' Pierce knew that she would never call him on his time off for anything short of an emergency.

'I'm sorry to interrupt your time away, Pierce, but Trevor Jacobs had a heart attack last night. The hospital called. Betty drove him there yesterday for the tests you requested and he suffered the episode in the waiting room. His children and grandchildren have arrived at the hospital and the attending doctor wondered if you might be able to head there later today. The whole family is worried the shock might be too much for his wife. I've taken the liberty of changing your flights to the earlier one. You'll need to be at Sydney airport in an hour and a half. I knew you'd want to be here.'

'Thanks, Tracy,' he said, swinging around to put his feet on the floor. 'Betty will be beside herself so we'll need to keep an eye on her. Tell the attending doctor I'll be there by lunchtime.' With that he ended the call.

'Is everything okay? Laine asked, sitting up in the bed and twisting her hair away from her face and into an untidy plait. 'Is it a patient?'

'Yes, and it's serious so I'm sorry but we'll have to cut our stay short by a few hours and take an earlier flight. I need to be back there as soon as possible.'

They drove back to Sydney and caught the next flight to Uralla. Pierce was preoccupied with Trevor and decided to leave their talk until that night. He invited her to dinner at his place, where he planned on telling her how he felt over a candlelit meal.

Their time away had been wonderful beyond belief and Laine thought he was the most amazing man but he was a country doctor who loved his life in Australia and she was a photographer with a life wherever she was booked. She had already broken two rules she had never broken before, and having dinner tonight would be breaking her no-second-date rule. And she already had doubts. She couldn't keep breaking her rules or she would have nothing to hold onto. Her rules protected her. They were her constant. If she broke the final rule and allowed this fling to turn into a relationship she risked everything. She risked her heart. That was something she couldn't do.

'I'll call and pick you up as soon as I've checked on my patient,' he said, kissing her cheek before she alighted from the car.

She was still happy inside that she had got to know the real Pierce and that he too knew more about her, but it was a bittersweet happiness. 'You should get going,' she finally muttered, and leant in to give him the last kiss she knew they would ever share. It was warm and tender and it made her want to cry. Pierce was a good man and he would make someone happy one day. He would have a family and a wonderful life but it wouldn't be with her. She already felt as if she needed him in her own life, and it had to stop—immediately.

'I'll see you tonight,' he said huskily as his lips left the softness of hers.

She didn't answer him.

Her walls were slowly being built up again and it was a quite conscious move on her part. She needed to block him out. She needed to protect herself. She had been stupid and reckless in letting Pierce in and thinking that she would be all right. Being in Toowoon Bay had not been the real world. It had been a beautiful dream and she had just woken up.

Standing outside her door, watching the man who had stolen her heart drive away, she knew she would leave today before he returned. She wasn't strong enough to love another person and let the universe play Russian roulette with her heart. But she doubted if she found herself in his bed again that night that she would be strong enough to leave. It was only lunchtime. She would head to Armidale, finish the shoot at the bank and catch the plane that afternoon. It might hurt him that she was gone without saying goodbye but it was what she needed to do.

Pierce arrived at the hospital fifteen minutes later to find Trevor's family gathered outside ICU where he had been transferred.

'Tell us what's happening,' Trevor's eldest son pleaded. 'I don't understand the medical mumbo-jumbo. We didn't know Dad even had a heart condition. He kept it from all of us. Is he going to make it?'

'Let me speak with the cardiologist and I'll let you know.' He paused and not able to see Betty, he asked the young man, 'How's your mother handling this?'

'Her granddaughters are distracting her but we're worried about them both. They're inseparable. Forty years of marriage and even though Dad's a grumpy old man at times, they've never had a cross word. She won't be able to go on without him.'

'Let's hope that's not something she has to contemplate. Keep a watch on your mother and I'll let you know in a few minutes how your father is getting on,' Pierce said, patting the man's back before hastily entering ICU after washing his hands. There he met the attending physician, Eric Milburn, who Pierce knew socially.

'Hi, Pierce, the family are all extremely anxious, as you've probably seen.'

'Yes, they're wanting me to update them. What's the prognosis?'

'Late last night I would have said grim and that's why we called the family here as we didn't think he would make it through the night. Somehow he's managed to turn a corner. We're all baffled, to be honest, but very pleased.'

Eric discussed at depth with Pierce the surgical intervention required as they worked though the case notes. It was nothing that Pierce had not seen before and he was elated at the news. He had arrived prepared to hear a dire prognosis. 'I'll let the family know.'

'Cautious optimism,' Eric told Pierce, as he removed his gloves and left ICU. 'And he will still be hospitalised for quite a few weeks with the surgery he has ahead.'

Pierce thanked Eric and left to speak to the family. Betty was now standing with her sons, awaiting the news of her husband.

'The doctors need to monitor your husband closely after his heart attack, and it's hospital procedure if there's the slightest indication of any injury to the heart to keep a patient in ICU.'

'How long will he stay here?' she asked, her face dressed with worry.

'It depends on how his coronary arteries are functioning. They're the arteries supplying blood to your husband's heart. If they're not working properly then his heart can't work either. They are also assessing the damage to the heart that may have occurred during the heart attack.'

'And how bad do they think it is?' the eldest son asked.

'Luckily, because he was already at the hospital and seen immediately, his chances of recovery are quite good, but he will need a stent to keep the walls of the coronary artery open and allow the blood to pass through.'

'When will that happen?' asked the taller of Betty's sons.

'They will ensure he is stable then schedule the surgery. Once your father has recovered completely from the operation and the cardiologist is satisfied, he will go home. He will need lots of rest. I will insist on that, but you all need to take the next few days slowly. It's been a shock to you all. I'll speak to you as soon as I know anything more. I'll update you and go over everything, including the recovery plan for home.'

The family had a lot to take in and there was still a long road ahead for their father but they thanked Pierce for his part in sending Trevor to hospital for testing.

'Thank you from the bottom of my heart,' Betty said, with tears running down her softly wrinkled cheeks. 'If you hadn't insisted on him having the tests, we might have lost him.'

'Trevor did the right thing and followed my instructions, so you can also give credit to him and the hospital for Trevor's prognosis. Of course, there's still a way to go. You may have a few more hurdles in store, but his spirit and the love he has out here will give him the best chance of making a great recovery.'

* * *

After leaving Trevor, Pierce checked in on James and found that he was stable. Myles was hoping to wean him off the ventilator within a few days. Now satisfied with the progress of both of his hospitalised patients, Pierce turned his attention to Laine. She was a wonderful woman and he intended to tell her that and more when he held her in his bed that night.

Laine's plane was due to touch down in Sydney at around the time she knew that Pierce would be arriving to collect her. The bank had agreed to the shoot being brought forward and she was able to wrap it up in just over an hour. Then with another hour to spare she headed to the airport, stopping to mail a letter before she dropped off her hire car and boarded the plane. Her heart was heavy as she sat on the small runway in the plane that would take her away from Pierce for ever.

It was for the best, she kept reminding herself. She had been single for a very long time and for good reason. The thought of caring for another person scared her to the core. Her hands were shaking and she hid her tears behind her sunglasses. Only the night before she had shared this man's bed but in the light of day she had panicked. The reality had been too much for her. She admitted to herself she was a coward when it came to love. Although she wished it to be different, she wasn't brave enough to risk heartbreak. She buckled her seatbelt, knowing there was no other way. As the plane picked up speed down the runway, Laine closed her eyes and prayed she would not live to regret leaving this town, and this man.

* * *

After leaving the hospital, Pierce headed to the jewellery store, where he looked for something special. Immediately he spied the stunning platinum chain with a solitaire diamond drop. It was perfect. The shop assistant gift-wrapped the piece and Pierce was on his way to the woman he knew had won his heart. The feelings he had for Laine were real and he intended on letting her know. A puzzled frown crossed his brow when he saw her rental car was missing from the motel car park. Pulling up outside her room, he dialled her number but her phone was switched off so he made his way to the motel office.

'Miss Phillips checked out this afternoon. It must have been just after lunch.'

Pierce headed to Armidale, thinking perhaps she had changed the time of the shoot and she was planning on staying the night with him. No point in keeping her motel room when she clearly wouldn't need it. He smiled to himself. Ever the consummate professional, her phone was probably turned off while she was working. The drive took fifteen minutes, and after parking behind the bank he walked along the side street with a smile a mile wide.

He had to admit he was in love. It had happened faster than he'd thought possible. But it had happened. This crazy, independent woman from the other side of the world had stolen his heart as quick as lightning. She was self-sufficient, opinionated, feisty, mysterious and challenging in so many ways. But she was also the one for him.

Entering the bank, his face fell when he saw there was no sign of her. No lighting, no equipment, no Laine.

'She left about an hour ago,' the bank manager told him. 'She brought the shoot forward, said she had an afternoon flight to catch.'

Laine didn't switch on her phone when she entered the Sydney terminal. She knew that Pierce would try to call. Most likely demand an explanation and attempt to talk her out of her decision to end it before it had really begun. It was easier if he just got the letter. No man before Pierce had ever made her question being alone and she didn't know if she could give him a good enough reason. The letter would put everything in perspective and he couldn't make her doubt her decision if she never heard the warmth in his voice again.

Pierce raced to the airport, desperate to see her. To find out what had happened. Her phone was still switched off so he knew there must be an emergency, a reason for her sudden departure. He couldn't fathom that she wouldn't just leave without an explanation.

Numb best described his mood as he left the airport twenty minutes later, knowing that Laine really had caught the afternoon flight. The kiosk attendant told him that she'd sold the stunning brunette a coffee before her one-thirty flight. She confirmed it was the same stunning woman who had flown in five days before with a trolley load of equipment. The airline staff weren't allowed to confirm it was her but it didn't take much to work it out. Laine had left town without so much as a goodbye.

As he lay in bed alone that night he knew that a farewell call would never come. Sydney was less than an hour's flight. They had shared that flight together that morning. There could be no emergency that wouldn't allow her to call and let him know. He realised she had breezed in and out of his life and there was nothing he could do. Nothing he would do.

He had fallen in love with a beautiful woman with a life and successful career overseas and for some insane reason he'd thought they would have a future together. That was not going to happen. He was suited to living in Uralla whereas Laine, he knew in his heart, was not. She was a woman with no ties and the world at her feet. She had a way of life and an attitude that was more in line with a big city. He could call but he wouldn't. Laine had switched off her phone for a reason. And he would accept it. He had to face the cold, hard fact that a country doctor would have no long-term appeal to a woman like Laine. And he didn't want his old life back. He liked his life just the way it was. New York was no place for him and apparently Laine felt the same about Uralla.

She had made her decision and looking at the diamond pendant on the dresser he knew he had to let her go.

CHAPTER ELEVEN

THE INVITATION FOR the gala ball and launch of the 'General Practitioners of Australia' calendar in Sydney arrived in the mail early one September morning and tugged at Pierce's heart just a little. It had been almost eight months since Laine had left and not a day went by when Pierce did not think about her.

He knew in time he would stop and some days he came close but then something would remind him of the stunning brunette who had crept under his skin and into his heart. Casual talk of Toowoon Bay by a friend, the mention of New York in passing, the sight of the ladder he'd climbed the day they'd first met…anyone holding a camera.

He'd had no choice but to let her go. She wasn't interested in a relationship with a country GP. And Pierce did not want to step back into the limelight that he had left behind. They had different priorities.

'Not interested,' Pierce muttered, as he threw the gilt-edged invitation in the bin and returned to the computer screen and his emails.

He had been expecting the invitation. His business manager, on Pierce's instructions, had contacted the charity and offered the use of Sydney's newest hotel at no cost to host the event. It was a hotel that Pierce owned. An investment that the business manager had convinced Pierce to make six months before when the original investors had needed to sell. It had been nearing completion when they'd run short on finance and there had been a concern it would sit as an eyesore on the Sydney skyline if it wasn't completed.

Pierce had agreed to take it on but wanted nothing to do with the running of it. He doubted he would even visit. It would give a good return and help fund his charities so that was all the level of his involvement until it came time to name it.

Pierce had thought long and hard about it. He had seen the photos. The hotel had an elegant yet strong façade. It was nothing like any other hotel on the harbour. Luxurious, yet almost minimal. Understated and timeless. The only hotel with a helipad for a discreet escape. He knew there was only one name it could carry, the one person he knew who personified the hotel. And so it became The Lainesway Hotel.

'Not interested in what?' Tracy asked as she entered the room to put a new disposable covering over the examination bed.

'Nothing. Nothing at all.'

'Fine, don't tell me,' she replied. 'But I think you need to get out. Come to our place for dinner on the weekend. Sitting here talking to yourself is not a good sign.'

'Then perhaps you could send the next patient in and I will have someone to speak to.'

'Trevor cancelled.'

'Why?' Pierce asked firmly. 'It's important I still

monitor him. I don't want him getting cocky on me and letting his appointments slip.'

'I told him that and he'll be in to see you tomorrow first thing. Apparently the *New England Focus* magazine is over there now, doing a photo shoot of the giant dolls' house he built for his granddaughters and also one to auction for the cardiac unit annual fundraiser. They are doing a feature story. It's taken him the best part of six months but the houses are magnificent.

'Fine, but if he cancels again, I will personally drive over and bring him here.'

'Don't worry, I told him that he's on your radar and he won't get away with anything.' Tracy laughed. 'But back to you talking to yourself—what was the topic of conversation? You didn't seem very happy.'

'Just the invitation to attend the calendar launch in Sydney. No way in hell am I going.'

'Why not? It sounds like fun. There might be some eligible women for the eligible doctors.'

No doubt, he thought, but more to the point there would be a certain photographer. He had no interest in seeing the woman whose name was emblazoned on the invitation: *World-famous photographer Laine Phillips.*

'I think you should go,' Tracy told him, as she bent down and collected the invitation from the recycle bin and began reading in earnest. 'Ooh, and it's at the The Lainesway Hotel. That's the lovely new hotel overlooking the Sydney Harbour. I read about it in the paper. It would be a lovely evening, you can get all gussied up and have an amazing time.'

'Is anything private any more?' he asked, taking the invitation back from her and tearing it into uneven strips before throwing it back in the bin.

'Come on, you might meet a nice lady. You need to be thinking about getting married and having children, and you clearly haven't tried to meet anyone around here.'

'I'm too busy.' Pierce continued typing and tried to ignore the direction of the conversation.

'You shouldn't be too busy for love,' Tracy said with a huge smile.

Pierce turned from the computer screen and stopped what he was doing. 'I don't think travelling to Sydney to be humiliated in a topless photograph will secure me a lifelong partner.'

'But it's for charity.'

'And?'

'Charity events bring out very nice people, it's a well-known fact, and one of them might be lovely enough to catch your eye.'

Pierce loved Tracy, always the optimist and now she was running around with a cupid's bow, trying to find him a wife. But try as he may, he couldn't imagine falling in love again. He'd thought he would be over Laine by now but he wasn't. He thought he was going mad some nights as he lay in his bed, thinking over in his head about their time together.

The anger had passed, and so too had the denial. He'd quickly realised Laine wasn't coming back. It had all been said so eloquently but so coldly in her letter that had arrived the day after she'd left town. In it she'd explained that although she'd had a wonderful few days it had been nothing more than that. A wonderful few days. She hoped he hadn't read any more into it and she apologised if she had led him on in any way. The letter had finished by telling him that she would always think fondly of him.

The letter had hit the wall in a crumpled ball. It had been seven months and twenty five days before the glossy invitation had arrived in the mail. Not that Pierce had been counting the days since she'd left.

'What was the charity again?' Tracy enquired, as she took the seat where the patients would normally sit during a consultation.

'Foster Children's Transition Programme.' Pierce eyed her becoming comfortable in the chair and wasn't sure if he liked that idea. It suggested a motherly advice session he didn't want or need.

'That's a wonderful cause, you should consider supporting it.

'I did,' Pierce retorted. 'I posed for the ridiculous calendar, remember?'

'I knew you were posing but I never met the photographer. She'd left before I arrived that day and you did the other shoots away from here and you never seemed to want to talk about it,' she announced, her voice not hiding her disappointment in not being included. 'But it's a very worthwhile cause. Our close friends fostered a child many years ago. The Phillips family, they lived in our street.'

Pierce stopped what he was doing at the mention of the name.

'Yes, Maisey and Arthur Phillips. They fostered a little girl for a short time and then finally adopted her. She was a real sweetie and the apple of her father's eye. They couldn't have children of their own but anyone would have thought she was their own flesh and blood, the way Arthur treated her. He taught her all about photography when she was growing up. It was his hobby and he had the biggest collection of cameras of anyone I knew. She'd run around town taking pictures of anything she could.'

'Yes, well, it's a small world. The photographer for my shoot, Laine Phillips, was their daughter,' he said, drawing a deep breath and speaking matter-of-factly so his voice did not betray his emotion.

'What was her name?' she asked.

'Laine. She shortened it from Melanie when she left town.'

Tracy paused as she pictured her angelic face as a child. 'Melanie Phillips was here?'

'Yes, in the flesh, but she didn't want anyone to know. She liked to keep to herself. Too many memories, or so she said.'

Tracy sighed. 'That's sad. I know everyone would love to see her. I'm surprised that she wasn't recognised.'

'I don't know what she looked like then but now she's...' He paused, thinking about her beautiful face, her smile, the way her long brown hair had spread across his pillow that morning. 'She's a stunning woman. She might not be the girl you all remember.'

'Why do you say that?'

'Quite the big city attitude. Think she's outgrown Uralla. But I gather she was looking for bigger and better when she left town as a teenager. Outgrew it then so it definitely wouldn't hold any appeal now.'

'She didn't *outgrow* it, Pierce. She left after her parents died. Maisey and Arthur were killed in a car accident about twelve years ago, when Melanie was only sixteen. We were all worried sick about her and we tried to rally round and help her out but she wouldn't have a bar of it.

'Almost overnight she changed personality from happy and outgoing to fiercely independent. She shut us all out. It was like the shutters came down on her heart and there was no way in. That was one of the saddest times for the town and then even sadder is the fact that Melanie just took off a few weeks later and no one's ever heard from her since. Nothing. It's like she fell off the planet.'

The words hit him in the chest. So she had run away from loss in Uralla just as he had done from his loss in New York. They were more alike than he'd realised. It was her way of dealing with sadness. To run away and pretend she'd never cared. It all fitted into place like a jigsaw but it didn't solve anything if he didn't do something about it.

'Tracy, can you book two seats on a plane to Sydney for the first Friday in October?' he said, after confirming the date on the almost unreadable invitation. 'I think I might just head over for the calendar launch after all. Will you be my date?'

'That sounds wonderful. So you want me to RSVP for you?'

'No, I think I'll decline as a calendar model, but I'd like you to buy two guest tickets. I don't want the fuss. I'd prefer to just melt into the background and watch the proceedings.'

Tracy wheeled her carry-on luggage off the plane and down the air bridge into the bustle of the terminal. It was just one night so her evening dress, shoes and accessories were all inside the one bag.

'I'm so excited!' she exclaimed as they hurriedly made their way to the cab rank. Pierce loaded her bag in the trunk of the cab, along with his suit bag containing his black tuxedo and a small leather carry-on.

'The Lainesway Hotel, please.'

'But the dinner isn't for hours. Aren't we going to our hotel first?' Tracy asked.

'About that,' Pierce replied. 'I saw you booked a very nice hotel but I changed the booking. We're staying at The Lainesway. And I have booked us each a suite. No arguments, you deserve to be spoilt.'

'But I was trying to be economical.'

'And I love you for it…but economical is not the way I want to tonight to play out.'

Tracy had settled into her suite when there was a knock at the door.

'Who is it?'

'Pierce. May I speak with you for a minute? I need you to do something for me.'

Tracy opened the door and invited him in. 'Do you need something pressed?'

Pierce smiled as he crossed the carpeted floor to a modern-style chaise longue by the huge floor-to-ceiling window. Gold silk drapes framed the view of the Sydney Opera House jutting out into the blue harbour waters. 'Ever the mother, aren't you? But the answer is, no, I don't need you to do anything before the gala. I need you to do something at the gala.'

'What would that be?' she asked, sitting on the edge of her bed where her long black beaded evening dress was draped.

'I'm not sure if you know that there will be an auction of the twelve framed calendar shots this evening, with the proceeds going to the charity.'

'No, I didn't, but that's a good way to generate more funds. It does sound like such a worthy cause. When I think of Melanie and all she went though as a child before she moved to Uralla, it breaks my heart.'

Pierce suddenly wondered if Laine was in her suite yet and if she was looking at the same view. And was she thinking about their time together? She was incredibly independent and distant at times, but underneath her armour she was loving and caring and scared. He just needed to make her understand that a life and love like they could share was worth the risk.

'I said that's a good idea.' Tracy had raised her voice a little to bring Pierce back from his reverie. She was puzzled by his behaviour but decided not to ask too many questions and accepted that he obviously had a lot on his mind.

'Yes, yes, it's a great marketing idea,' he said, standing up and moving away from the window. 'Anyway, I would like you to buy them for me.'

'All of them?'

'Yes, all twelve.'

'And exactly how much is that going to set me back? You pay me well but I don't think well enough for that.'

Pierce laughed. 'No, what I should have said was *on my behalf*. I will be giving you a cheque for the amount I wish to pay at auction and it's well above what they would be expecting. There shouldn't be any competition from other bidders.'

Tracy suddenly wore a puzzled expression. 'Any reason why you would want to hang pictures of yourself and eleven other doctors you don't know in our office?'

Pierce shook his head and grinned. 'I don't want to keep any of them. I'm happy to give them away. Perhaps the nurses at the hospital can take one each, except mine. That can be boxed up somewhere, never to be seen again.'

'Then why exactly do you want to buy them if you don't want them?'

'It's for a good cause.'

Tracy knew better than to delve further. Pierce was a lovely man but there were some parts of his life he guarded and clearly this was one of them. She checked her watch and then went to the luxurious marble bathroom to run a bath. 'I think I'll soak for a while. I don't often have the time to take a bubble bath but it's quite a special night tonight so I'm going to spoil myself. There's still over an hour until cocktails,' she called out over the sound of the running water. 'You can just leave the cheque on the desk and I'll bring it down with me.'

Pierce pulled the bank cheque from his inside jacket pocket. 'It's here by your purse.'

Tracy returned to the bedroom to collect her make-up and while she was there she picked up the cheque. 'I'll do it now so I don't forget...' She paused to read the details and her voice became a shrill scream. 'Are you mad? One point two million dollars for some photographs?'

'I know it seems a lot...'

'It doesn't *seem* a lot,' she replied. 'It *is* a lot and it's mad. Photographs of people you don't even know for that much money. I wouldn't pay that much for photos signed by the entire Royal family...and I adore the monarchy!'

'Look, I don't have time to go into everything now,

you need to get ready for tonight and I don't want to rush you so I'm going to leave. You have the cheque so I will meet you downstairs in an hour and a quarter, and can you please bid for the photographs?'

'A million dollars?' she declared, still in shock as she walked in to turn off her bath.

'Yes, a million dollars for a worthy cause, and don't worry, I can afford it. I have money put away for a rainy day,' he called to her.

Tracy walked back into the room with her arms folded across her chest. 'I'm not worried about the money, I know you can well afford it. I'm worried about the reason behind it.'

Pierce was taken aback by her comment. 'What do you mean by "I know you can well afford it"?'

Tracy sat on the edge of the bed and clasped her hands in her lap. 'Pierce, do you honestly think that my husband would have sold his practice to you and let you take over the care of his patients without knowing everything there was to know about you? He loves the people of this town and he wanted to hand them over to someone who would do the right thing by them. He had to be sure.'

'But neither of you ever asked me about my past or my money.'

'There was nothing we needed to ask you. Gregory made enquiries before you arrived. We might be country folk but we're not silly. You were the son of a very wealthy parents who died when you were a child, you attended a private boarding school in Germany from the age of ten until seventeen, when you returned to Sydney and to study medicine. You were well respected by your peers and your grades were exemplary. When

you arrived in Uralla two years ago you didn't bring up
your family or any of what we knew so we didn't either.

'My husband believes you judge the man on his
own merits, not his family money. You were a great
young doctor and just what the people of the town
needed. There was nothing shady in your past, just a
lot of money. To be honest, we weren't sure if you had
given it away or something had happened because you
hardly live an extravagant life here in town, although
we did notice a lot of anonymous donations to the local
schools after you arrived. Perhaps a coincidence,' she
said, looking directly at him, 'but we think not. You're
a good doctor, who always buys a lot of raffle tickets
and fundraising lamingtons, that's all that matters here.'

Pierce was flabbergasted. 'I can't believe you never
said a thing in all this time. No one in the town knows?
Or is everyone aware and not saying anything?'

'No one knows and it's not their business. You're
just the nice young doctor who everyone respects and
trusts, and that's all they need to know. You don't flash
your money around, well, not until tonight anyway. So
how would anyone know? It won't come from me or
Gregory, so unless you suddenly turn up with a flashy
imported sports car, the town will never know.'

Pierce was still in shock. His secret had been kept by
them for the last two years and he'd had no idea. The
day was certainly not as he had expected but nothing
about his life had been since Laine Phillips had come
to Uralla. She had turned his life upside down and now
he wanted to turn hers around and make her understand
that real love was worth the risk.

'Okay, we can talk later. But now I'll leave you to
soak and I'll meet you downstairs in an hour.

* * *

Pierce stood in the doorway of the ballroom dressed in a black tuxedo with satin lapels, a crisp white shirt and black bow-tie. His black hair was slicked back and his skin freshly shaven. The grand ballroom of The Lainesway Hotel was at capacity with over five hundred guests. The event organisers had done their work in publicising the night.

His gaze slowly, purposefully roamed his surroundings. Twelve stunning crystal chandeliers hung in the grandeur of the softly lit room. The walls were appointed with Tasmanian pine and sophisticated fabric panels. Huge white and black floral centrepieces with steps of tealights decorated each table. Then he saw her. Like a Grecian goddess she moved through the crowd. Her floor-length one-shouldered white dress was trimmed with gold stones and it caught the light. Her long dark hair had been twisted into a chignon at the nape of her neck. She was breathtaking.

Although he wanted to approach, he decided to leave their meeting until the auction so he took his allocated seat at a table with Tracy.

The fundraising auction for the twelve calendar framed prints began shortly after main course. All were signed by the photographer and being put up for auction individually. They were on easels across the stage but each was hidden from view with a black covering.

'I thought we might have some fun—mix it up and start with December then work our way backwards,' the auctioneer announced, with Laine standing by his side. 'Each of the doctors is here tonight and has kindly agreed to step up to the stage during the auction and also to sign their print. That is, except our first lot tonight. Lot Twelve, Dr December. Dr Pierce Beaumont sent his apologies, so I'm sorry, ladies, he won't be here to sign this one, but we have the eleven other doctors.'

'I have been able to make it. I'm here,' Pierce called in a husky voice.

'So much for melting into the background,' Tracey muttered, as she sipped her champagne.

'Did I just hear something?' the auctioneer enquired, looking out to the audience.

Pierce stood and made his way through the tables to the stage.

Looking directly at Laine, he answered, 'There's nowhere else I'd rather be than here tonight.'

Laine froze. Her heart began to race. She'd had no idea Pierce would be attending. Her acceptance to attend had been given on the assurance that he had declined.

Pierce made his way to the stairs and then took his place beside Laine and his photograph.

'I thought you weren't coming,' she managed to mutter, without meeting his gaze, her heart racing so fast she thought she would pass out.

'I wasn't but then curiosity got the better of me. I thought I'd like to see which photo you chose. Was it at the McKenzies' property or perhaps me perched atop the ladder?'

Pierce watched Laine's eyes narrow as the auctioneer crossed to the easel. She wouldn't look in the direction of her work, and she seemed very nervous. Pierce had no idea why until the auctioneer slowly lifted the dust

cover and the photograph was revealed. Laine hadn't
chosen any of the staged photographs. Instead, she had
enlarged and framed one from their day in the rainforest, taken only hours before they'd made love. It wasn't
a planned shot, there was no posing or design. It was as
spontaneous as the moment she'd slipped into the pool
and into his arms.

Their time away had meant something to her. This
was the proof he needed.

'Well, it seems that all the framed photographs will
indeed be signed tonight,' the auctioneer said with a
cough to clear his throat. 'So I'll start the bidding for
Dr Pierce Beaumont at five hundred dollars.

A very elegant, manicured hand went up to the right
of the room. 'Five hundred.'

'Five it is,' the auctioneer announced.

Another French-manicured hand was raised. 'Six
hundred dollars.'

'Six hundred I'm bid.'

A third female hand was raised. 'One thousand.'

'I'll take one thousand from the lady with the lovely
voice at the back.'

'One hundred thousand dollars.'

The room fell silent for a moment then burst into
noise. Those closest, who had heard Tracy's bid,
gasped. Those who hadn't been listening started chat-
ting wildly amongst themselves, trying to understand
what was causing such a reaction. Trying to catch up
with what had just happened.

Laine's eyes widened in shock.

'Did I hear correctly? Did someone just bid one hundred thousand dollars?' the auctioneer asked loudly, the wooden gravel in his hand.

'Yes,' Tracy replied. 'One hundred thousand dollars per photograph, and I want all twelve. I can give you a cheque for one point two million now.'

Tracy had never done anything that exciting in her life and she blushed a little when she realised the entire room was looking at her. She nodded and acknowledged the attention.

Pierce stood smiling on the stage next to the unveiled photo. He hoped his generous donation would kick-start the rest of Sydney society into opening their cheque books. He knew that many there were spurred on by the need to outdo each other so he hoped he had set the bar high enough that all of the foster transition centres would be funded by the evening's donations from the well-heeled guests. If not, he would cover them himself anyway.

He posed for the media after signing the photograph then turned to speak to Laine. But she was gone. As quickly as she had appeared on the stage, she had disappeared. Pierce looked everywhere but she had left the ballroom.

Immediately he called for the event co-ordinator and questioned her about Laine's whereabouts.

'She wanted to be alone. She's on the rooftop.'

'The rooftop?'

'Yes, it's a secure area. There's a door that leads to the rooftop from the eighteenth floor stairwell but unfortunately I gave her my only pass, but I can give hotel security a call and get another one. I'll be right back.'

Pierce watched as she walked away but then as an afterthought added, 'Miss Laine has booked a helicopter to collect her from the rooftop and take her to a large private yacht in fifteen minutes. She has a photographic assignment on board for the next two weeks. It's anchored just out of the harbour and due to sail at midnight.'

CHAPTER TWELVE

PIERCE DIDN'T WAIT for the co-ordinator to contact Security. He made the call himself. They sent one of the guards, and on learning that Pierce was the owner of the hotel, the guard accompanied him to the stairwell and to the rooftop door, but as they tried to open it they found it was jammed.

'It's as if there's something leaning against it,' the guard said with a puzzled look on his face. 'Definitely won't be anyone going out this way tonight.'

'Is there another way?' Pierce asked, not bothering to hide his desperation to get to Laine in time.

Rubbing his chin, the guard looked at Pierce. 'It's that important?'

'Nothing more important in the world right now.'

'Then come with me.'

The guard took Pierce in the opposite direction and they climbed down two flights of stairs until they came to another secure doorway. The guard again used his pass to open the door that led onto a balcony.

'And now exactly where are we and why are we here?' Pierce asked, as he stood in the cool breeze on a balcony sixteen floors above the street. He didn't care to look down, preferring to look across the lights of the city skyline and then lifting his gaze upwards to the darkened sky now strung with stars.

'Well, just around here is a fire escape,' the guard began, as he walked with Pierce slightly to their left. 'It leads to the rooftop and the helipad.'

Pierce followed the young man and quickly came across a black metal ladder attached to the rendered wall. Pierce studied it carefully and noticed it had bolts every six inches holding the framework in place. It was his only way to Laine. Looking at his watch, he knew that there was less than ten minutes until the helicopter arrived. He tilted his head to see the end of the fire escape. He assumed that was the rooftop and where Laine was waiting for her lift to the yacht.

'Are you okay, climbing the fire escape?' the security guard asked.

'I guess I've run out of other options,' Pierce answered, without looking away from the framework he was about to ascend.

'She must be very special. Not sure I'd be doing it.'

Pierce turned his gaze to the uniformed man. 'Very special.' And with that Pierce removed his tuxedo jacket, undid his bow-tie and the top button of his shirt and put his foot on the first rung of the ladder. His stomach churned and his heart raced as he lifted his weight to the next rung. His hands held tightly to the sides of the framework, turning his knuckles white as pulled himself up yet another step. Pausing for a moment, he took a deep breath and kept her beautiful face in his mind as he continued the climb. Rung by rung he thought about Laine, of her laughing as they'd raced to the water's edge, the kiss he'd stolen just before the sun had risen on the farm, her lying naked in his bed.

He was going to reach her, come hell or high water.

Finally he reached the top and as he stepped onto the rooftop caught sight of her silhouette. She was standing alone, looking up into the sky.

Pierce cleared his throat. 'A penny for your thoughts.'

She spun on her heel to see Pierce standing on the rooftop.

She couldn't believe he was there. She had blocked the doorway to make sure he couldn't reach her. She didn't want to be that close to him again. Ever.

'What the hell are you doing up here?'

'Trying to convince you to give us a shot,' he replied, stepping carefully towards her. Looking across at the doorway, he noticed it was blocked by a planter. 'I wanted to tell you that eight months ago but you didn't give me a chance. You ran away, and tonight you blocked my way to reach you.'

Laine followed his eye line to the barred doorway. 'I didn't run away. I finished what I came to do and I left. But why are you here, and...*how*?' She stumbled over her words, aware that Pierce had found the only other way to reach her. He had climbed an outside fire escape on top of a multi-storey building. She wasn't sure how he'd done it. His fear of heights should have prevented him but somehow he'd managed. Somehow he hadn't let that fear cripple him. Somehow he had come to her despite his fear.

He walked across the rooftop to her and reach for her hands. 'Because I want you. And I wasn't about to let anything stop me.'

Laine tried to control her emotions but she was struggling. Each moment it became harder not to fall into his arms. But she couldn't. The helicopter would arrive any minute and she could leave him. And never look back.

'I told you how I felt in my letter. It was just a few days we shared, nothing more.'

'And the calendar photograph of me, how do you explain that?'

Laine pulled away but he caught her wrist, pulling her back to him.

'It was good lighting.' It was so much more and they both knew it. It had been her favourite. It had reminded her of an incredibly special time and she'd wanted the world to see it.

'That's the worst excuse ever. The lighting on any other photo would have been better and we both know it,' he said, looking intensely into her eyes. 'It was what happened a few hours later, wasn't it?'

'I liked the photo, let's leave it at that,' she replied in not more than a whisper, not daring to look at him.

'I'm not buying that. And I'll stay right here until I hear something that convinces me to go.'

'You're a wonderful man, but I don't want or need a relationship. I don't want to depend on someone.'

'Not someone, *me*. I want you to depend on me.'

She shook her head. Her walls were crumbling. She felt the months apart vanishing in the warmth of his touch and it frightened her. 'I can't, I'm not brave enough. Pierce, I'm not worth it, just let me go.'

'That's where you are wrong,' he told her, his hands holding hers even more tightly. 'You are worth it, and so much more, too.'

Laine felt tears welling in her eyes and spilling down her face. No man had ever wanted to risk everything to love her. She was finding it more difficult by the second not to accept his words. He had overcome a huge obstacle to be standing there with her. Maybe he had enough belief for both of them but even if she could take her fear out of the equation there were practical barriers too. 'I have no idea how *we* could work, it's not even close to feasible. Are you forgetting that I live in another country? In a city you hate. A city that brings back memories you can't live with.'

'I can put memories where they belong but I can't live knowing you're somewhere without me. Memories we both need to put to rest are keeping us apart. We can build new happy memories together. We can both let go of the past safe in the knowledge we have each other. Eight months have passed and I don't love you any less than the day you woke in my arms. In fact, I think I love you more.'

'That's ridiculous,' she said, pulling her hands from his and walking away. Looking out across the water, she could see the lights of the harbour and the yacht moored waiting for her. 'We barely knew each other then.'

'Then tell me, if you didn't feel anything, why did you run away from me? Why couldn't you say good-bye to my face?'

Laine knew what Pierce said was true. She had been falling for him then and not a day had gone by that she hadn't thought back to the time, however brief, that they had shared together. Maybe he was right, maybe it *was* love, but she was scared. So scared that it would end and she would be left alone, her heart broken all over again. She had nothing to lose in telling him the truth so she turned to face him. Her expression told the story.

'I was scared, Pierce. There, I said it. I was scared then, and I'm scared now. I'm frightened to my core that you will leave one day, that something might take you away from me. I couldn't bear to be without you, to be alone again.'

'And what are you now?' he demanded. 'You're *alone*, Laine. You had me, you still have my heart, but you're alone. We wake up without each other and you go to sleep without each other. How could it be worse than that?'

'But I never really had you, it was only a weekend.'

'A wonderful weekend that we could turn into a life-time if you'll let it happen. I'm admitting that I love you and I think you might just love me,' he said, reaching for her hands again and holding them tightly in the strength of his own. 'If you didn't love me just a little then you wouldn't have chosen that photograph and you wouldn't have run away and you wouldn't be shaking right now.'

Laine looked away in silence. All of it was true.

'And you wouldn't be crying…'

Pierce smiled and using the softness of his hand he wiped away another tear as it trickled across her cheek then gently cupped her face as he looked into her eyes.

'I don't want to live without you. I can't. The last eight months have been empty. My life has been empty but I didn't know it until I met you. You challenge me, you make me feel alive, and I want you more than any woman I've ever met. I can practise anywhere in the world and you can take photographs anywhere. The possibilities are endless—we just have to decide what suits us. And our children.'

'Children? How do you know I even want children?'

'Because you have devoted your life to helping them. We can foster, we can adopt and even throw in a few of our own. But that's much later. What do you say? Maybe we can pass on the wedding for the time being if it's too much too soon, just live with me. Wake up in my arms and make me the happiest man alive.'

Laine's head was spinning. Suddenly, looking at the man standing before her, she realised she was about to be just as crazy as Pierce had been moments ago when he'd climbed the fire escape. Maybe he was right, maybe she *was* ready to be loved. And to love him back.

She closed her eyes and suddenly knew that what she was about to do was the right thing. She had no choice, her heart was overruling her past and his heart was putting it where it belonged, drowning out her doubt and convincing her to take the leap of faith and give in to love. He had shown her how to be brave.

She stood on tiptoe and kissed him. 'I'm not exactly sure how we'll sort out the practicalities but we will if you love me.'

Pierce pulled her into his arms and kissed her and then kissed her some more.

'My love for you is greater than you will ever know. I didn't come here with an empty promise. I want you to know you can trust me, lean on me and know I'm never leaving your side for the rest of my life.'

He swept her into his arms, pulling her body even closer to him. Brushing away the tendrils of her hair that had fallen across her face, he kissed her the way he intended to do for the rest of their lives.

And for the first time in her life, and over the sound of the helicopter approaching, Laine said the words *I love you*.

EPILOGUE

'THE HOME IS AMAZING,' Laine said, her eyes bright with excitement. Slowly, taking in every detail, she surveyed the ground floor of the accommodation for foster-children transitioning from home care when they turned eighteen. 'Thank you, Pierce. It's more than I had ever dreamed possible.'

'You, my darling wife, are more than welcome. Your dreams are my dreams and I have the means to make them all come true.'

'I know that now, but there are many men in the world who wouldn't share their wealth the way you so willingly do with others in need.'

Laine walked over to one of the huge murals that decorated the inside walls. Pierce had commissioned a group of street artists to paint inside the three-storey building with colourful and uplifting work that would make the new residents feel at home.

'I absolutely love this,' she said, before she rushed off to look at the other rooms. Pierce had designed the interior layout and she had done the decorating, except for the mural, which was a surprise.

There were study rooms filled with desks and computers, a games area, a laundry, a commercial-size kitchen where the residents could hone their cooking skills, a home theatre and a huge dining room where everyone could eat their evening meal together like a big extended family. Each young person had their own room and was responsible for their own laundry and there were kitchen rosters. It had not been designed as a holiday home but a real home with rules and responsibilities. Trained house mothers and fathers would provide guidance and counselling to these young adults to help them on their pathway in life.

'This is one of the happiest days of my life,' she announced, as she walked back to her husband filled with pride at what they had accomplished together.

'This is just the beginning,' he told her, and pulled her into his arms. 'This is the pilot transition home, and once we gauge its success and make improvements where required, then we will begin the process of building one in each capital city. Australia can lead the way and this programme can be a model for others.'

Laine knew the excitement she heard in his voice was real. The project meant as much to Pierce as it did to her.

'You are the most generous, wonderful man in the world. I'm so proud of you,' Laine said, as she leant her head on her husband's shoulder and looked again at the community home they had built for at-risk teenagers.

'Not nearly as proud as I am of you, Mrs Beaumont,' he said, before he kissed her tenderly. 'I don't know how you do it. A working photographer, an interior decorator for this project, a mother of two foster-children and now one on the way!' His hand rested protectively on Laine's tiny bump, which was only just showing through her thin summer dress. 'And not to forget, the most loving wife. I am the luckiest man in the world.'

Looking in to the warmth of his smiling eyes, Laine felt her heart flutter as it always did when he held her. 'I think I'm the fortunate one, Pierce. You convinced me to break all my silly rules and now you have my heart for ever.'

* * * * *

Mills & Boon® Hardback

December 2014

ROMANCE

Taken Over by the Billionaire	Miranda Lee
Christmas in Da Conti's Bed	Sharon Kendrick
His for Revenge	Caitlin Crews
A Rule Worth Breaking	Maggie Cox
What The Greek Wants Most	Maya Blake
The Magnate's Manifesto	Jennifer Hayward
To Claim His Heir by Christmas	Victoria Parker
Heiress's Defiance	Lynn Raye Harris
Nine Month Countdown	Leah Ashton
Bridesmaid with Attitude	Christy McKellen
An Offer She Can't Refuse	Shoma Narayanan
Breaking the Boss's Rules	Nina Milne
Snowbound Surprise for the Billionaire	Michelle Douglas
Christmas Where They Belong	Marion Lennox
Meet Me Under the Mistletoe	Cara Colter
A Diamond in Her Stocking	Kandy Shepherd
Falling for Dr December	Susanne Hampton
Snowbound with the Surgeon	Annie Claydon

MEDICAL

Midwife's Christmas Proposal	Fiona McArthur
Midwife's Mistletoe Baby	Fiona McArthur
A Baby on Her Christmas List	Louisa George
A Family This Christmas	Sue MacKay

Mills & Boon® Large Print
December 2014

ROMANCE

HISTORICAL

MEDICAL

Mills & Boon® Hardback
January 2015

ROMANCE

The Secret His Mistress Carried	Lynne Graham
Nine Months to Redeem Him	Jennie Lucas
Fonseca's Fury	Abby Green
The Russian's Ultimatum	Michelle Smart
To Sin with the Tycoon	Cathy Williams
The Last Heir of Monterrato	Andie Brock
Inherited by Her Enemy	Sara Craven
Sheikh's Desert Duty	Maisey Yates
The Honeymoon Arrangement	Joss Wood
Who's Calling the Shots?	Jennifer Rae
The Scandal Behind the Wedding	Bella Frances
The Bridegroom Wishlist	Tanya Wright
Taming the French Tycoon	Rebecca Winters
His Very Convenient Bride	Sophie Pembroke
The Heir's Unexpected Return	Jackie Braun
The Prince She Never Forgot	Scarlet Wilson
A Child to Bind Them	Lucy Clark
The Baby That Changed Her Life	Louisa Heaton

MEDICAL

How to Find a Man in Five Dates	Tina Beckett
Breaking Her No-Dating Rule	Amalie Berlin
Happened One Night Shift	Amy Andrews
Tamed by Her Army Doc's Touch	Lucy Ryder

Mills & Boon® Large Print
January 2015

ROMANCE

The Housekeeper's Awakening	Sharon Kendrick
More Precious than a Crown	Carol Marinelli
Captured by the Sheikh	Kate Hewitt
A Night in the Prince's Bed	Chantelle Shaw
Damaso Claims His Heir	Annie West
Changing Constantinou's Game	Jennifer Hayward
The Ultimate Revenge	Victoria Parker
Interview with a Tycoon	Cara Colter
Her Boss by Arrangement	Teresa Carpenter
In Her Rival's Arms	Alison Roberts
Frozen Heart, Melting Kiss	Ellie Darkins

HISTORICAL

Lord Havelock's List	Annie Burrows
The Gentleman Rogue	Margaret McPhee
Never Trust a Rebel	Sarah Mallory
Saved by the Viking Warrior	Michelle Styles
The Pirate Hunter	Laura Martin

MEDICAL

200 Harley Street: The Shameless Maverick	Louisa George
200 Harley Street: The Tortured Hero	Amy Andrews
A Home for the Hot-Shot Doc	Dianne Drake
A Doctor's Confession	Dianne Drake
The Accidental Daddy	Meredith Webber
Pregnant with the Soldier's Son	Amy Ruttan

MILLS & BOON®

Why shop at millsandboon.co.uk?

Each year, thousands of romance readers find their perfect read at millsandboon.co.uk. That's because we're passionate about bringing you the very best romantic fiction. Here are some of the advantages of shopping at www.millsandboon.co.uk:

* **Get new books first**—you'll be able to buy your favourite books one month before they hit the shops

* **Get exclusive discounts**—you'll also be able to buy our specially created monthly collections, with up to 50% off the RRP

* **Find your favourite authors**—latest news, interviews and new releases for all your favourite authors and series on our website, plus ideas for what to try next

* **Join in**—once you've bought your favourite books, don't forget to register with us to rate, review and join in the discussions

Visit **www.millsandboon.co.uk**
for all this and more today!